FAR & AWAY

ISBN 978-1-880100-57-8

Russian Life Books
73 Main Street, Suite 402
Montpelier, VT 05601-0567
russianlife.com
orders@russianlife.com
phone 802-223-4955

FAR & AWAY

TALES FROM RURAL RUSSIA

By Varvara Buzina

Translated by Liv Bliss
Illustrated by Asya Lisina

russian life
BOOKS

CONTENTS

INTRODUCTION

Do you know what a village is, dear reader? Have you ever been in a Russian village?
Then follow me. There it stands – far from the city, deep in the forest, and made up
of a dozen little huts, no more.

Those huts, which could have come straight out of a fairytale, are log cabins with
an inside wall that divides the interior into two unequal parts, a smaller one that's not
heated and a larger one that is. In the larger part there'll be a stove, and in that stove,
in a cast-iron pot, potatoes are boiling, or a cabbage soup is simmering, or a duck is
slowly braising. Around the stove hang bunches of mushrooms, onions with braided
stalks, and herbs, for healing and for soup. Clay pots and little jars, containing kasha
groats or salt, perch on ledges, and frying pans, colanders, and ladles swing from nails
driven into the wall. In the corner is a pile of oven forks, from the very largest, to lift
cast-iron pots the size of buckets, to the smallest, for handling the little saucepans that
cook the kasha. The firewood lies in a tidy heap by the stove, and alongside there's a
hand-broom to sweep away the cobwebs, a poker to stir the burning wood, and an
iron shovel for cleaning out the burned residue. The stove has a sleeping ledge care-
lessly covered with an old sheepskin coat, and could anything be sweeter than to sleep
there as the winter wears on and the frozen forest sings its rustling song?

One corner of the hut, known as the holy corner, has shelves to hold icons (of
St. Nikolai the Wonder-Worker and the Mother of God, at least) and a flickering
icon lamp, and hiding behind the icons are government bond documents, birth
certificates, and newspaper clippings.

Peering into the sleeping area, we'll see a tall iron bedstead covered by straw-stuffed
mattresses, down comforters, and feather pillows. And there's always a rug on the
wall, with a woven design depicting swans on a pond or a handsome hero of Russian
folklore carrying a frightened princess away on the back of a huge gray wolf.

Back in the living space, a clock ticks on the wall, counting down the village's remaining time. The room smells of freshly hand-scraped wood, kitchen soap, stove fumes, and medicinal wormwood. Trunks store thick woolen jackets, socks, caps, and scarves against winter's return. A china cabinet displays tinkling shot glasses with gilded rims, gaudy cups, and ceramic figurines that are mostly girls wearing ornate headdresses or shouldering a bucket yoke. In a place of honor, covered with a doily, stands the television, where the villagers get all their news and watch the love stories that seem to go on forever, and their faith in that modern miracle is right up there with their faith in God.

In the unheated entryway reside empty jars for preserving and canning, old buckets, a jumble of household odds and ends – and the lady of the house wants it all, needs it all, and holds it all close to her heart. From there you can descend into the cellar, the repository of everything to dress up a table – potatoes, jars of pickled cucumbers, marinated mushrooms, sour cabbage, jams, stewed fruit, and homebrew. The cellar is life itself, and that's what the village is all about. We need no one, and we live better than the city folk live.

And in summer, we sit at a table in the garden, under an old apple tree, and fire up the samovar with pine cones. An acrid odor will float through the air, and the medallions on the samovar's golden flank will shine, and the wasps will hover over the jam, and we'll drink tea and crunch on crusty little bread rings, unwrap sticky candies, and think about maybe heading into the forest tomorrow. For raspberries. Or blueberries. Or strawberries.

Come with me, reader, come with me. Hurry, now. We're off to meet the folks who live here in our village, to learn how they build their stoves, do their laundry, tell their yuletide fortunes. We'll snoop on their lives, join them at milking time, scatter grain for the chickens, take a ride in a rickety old cart, and heat the banya.[1] I want to make you a gift of my village, the place I came to thirty years ago, leaving Moscow, the theater, and my life of creature comforts behind. But, believe me when I tell you that

---

1. The traditional Russian bath house, which plays a huge role in country life – not just as the place to scrub yourself, and sometimes your laundry, clean in various ingenious ways but also as a refuge from the world, somewhere to relax with people who won't mind seeing you naked. The village banya figures prominently in Russian folk magic, and appears so often in my stories as to become almost a character in its own right.

the village is a splendid place to be. All sorts of people live here, and they get themselves into the oddest predicaments. And in this book, you'll see that for yourself.

Before I go, I want to say thank you – a big, sincere, affectionate thank you – to Paul Richardson, long-time publisher of the fine magazine Russian Life, who has exercised infinite tact, year after year, in his dealings with all things Russian. No praise is high enough for the enthusiasm and love with which he invests his heart and his resources into this project that is so dear to us. I would also like to thank Maria Antonova, managing editor of Russian Life, for patiently nudging my stories in the right direction. And Liv Bliss, who has the hardest job of all, that of translation, and who has for many years been my co-author, since the English-speaking reader would not be able to understand a word of what I've written if she were not there to convey it all to them. And, of course, Asya Lisina, the irreplaceable illustrator of my stories, a marvelous artist with a clear vision of each tale I tell.

I have every hope that readers will find this book entertaining and that through it they will see the village as I do. Because I surely haven't lived here all this time without learning a thing or two. Or even three.

Varvara Buzina
Somewhere in the back of beyond, 2024

TRANSLATOR'S NOTE

When the journey that would lead to this book first began, two things quickly became clear. The first was that this was going to be the most challenging creative translation I had ever taken on. The second was that, despite being more than six thousand actual miles and a cultural and historical world apart, the author and I share a substantial expanse of common ground.

The challenges were quite plain to see: the realia of Russian village life and the oddities of the village idiom form a linguistic environment unlike any I had encountered in over forty years as a professional translator – a career that has so far encompassed a Bible-based screenplay, a medieval saga of Jewish valor, a sword and sandals whodunit, earnest biographies of Stanislavsky, Bulgakov, and members of the Soviet political pantheon, a fantasy complete with wood-gnomes and an eight-legged horse, and a tale of piratical time travel, among the fourteen books that I'll acknowledge having had anything to do with. Even King David and quasi-mythological heroes wielded readily researchable weapons and spoke standard Russian. None of this prepared me for the adventure I was about to embark on.

And the common ground? Oh, let me count the ways. In fact, there are so many that I have had to whittle the list down. I also live in a rural setting – not a village, but a small town that was a village not so long ago – and resonate with numerous recurrent themes in this book: the local eccentrics and troublemakers (sometimes the same individuals); the turn of the seasons, so challenging especially for those who aren't as young as they would like to be; the love/hate relationship with the seasonal visitors, their pockets full of cash and their presence inevitably disruptive to a more sleepy way of life; the complexities attendant on finding good medical care; the comparable complexities of tracking down a reliable (and preferably sober) handyman; and, most of all, the kind hearts beneath gruff exteriors. And in both author Varvara Buzina's experience and my own, the

"

outside world constantly impinges, bringing an awareness that the apparently solid underpinnings of village life are not only fragile but also fluid.

I, like the author, moved here later in life and would never have imagined this as my future, but I delight in it all and wouldn't have it any other way.

None of this is to say that my world and the world of Sheshurino and its nearby hamlets are interchangeable. Certainly not, for Russia has been cruelly marked by the Second World War and the Soviet past, upheavals that have divided families across generations, and by an economic meltdown to which that term does no justice. The Russian village, now as in Soviet times and in centuries before, has always had the short end of the stick. But with neighbors helping neighbors, an indomitable determination to make do in preference to doing without, and a sly ability to skirt or bend the rules (and get away with it), the people you will meet in this book survive and often even thrive.

This, then, was a match made in a peculiar kind of translation heaven. It may take a village to raise a child, but it certainly did take a sizable support squad to make the translations in this book. The help and guidance I have received along the way have made my work so much easier, and the result so much less embarrassing, than might otherwise have been. The delightful Varvara Buzina was unfailingly patient with my questions and prompt with her responses. Nora Favorov, translator and editor extraordinaire, offered many elegant alternatives and unfailingly highlighted choices I had made that would constitute cruel and unusual punishment for the reader. She and her husband Oleg also set me straight on points of fact and idiosyncrasies of language that I hadn't even realized were an issue. And Michael Ishenko, author, translator, and bilingual polymath, responded, comprehensively and with an innate understanding of my limitations, to every query I came up with before I had even consigned my draft translation to the screen. Finally, warm thanks are due to the irrepressible Paul Richardson, editor and publisher of *Russian Life*, who first came up with the idea that has culminated in this book.

The stories here are self contained and can be read in any order (although I do suggest beginning with the first; after that, it's reader's choice). Some characters will recur; others will appear only once. Here you will find moonshine (not the lunar kind), felt boots, herbs and potions, time-tested magic, the ubiquitous Russian village banya, generous servings of kvas,[1] problems with livestock, barnyard and domestic, the joys of rambunctious childhood and fresh-faced youth, the trials of a lonely old age. For the reader, there will be wry smiles, maybe a chuckle or two, perhaps a tear; for the translator, there has been the privilege and the pleasure of having helped bring these well-crafted little gems to the audience they deserve.

Liv Bliss
Arizona, 2024

---

1. A beverage similar in appearance to a good dark beer that is usually low in alcohol. Among an untold number of recipes, dried rye bread features as a staple in these stories.

SHESHURINO

The left side of Sheshurino, our little village, clings to Lake Nagovye, and the right side to a forest that's all downed trees and bogs. A glacier passed our way in the dim and distant past, leaving in its wake boulder-sized stones, sand, and lakes like platters of spotless sky.

The woods are flush with wild strawberries and bilberries, the bogs with cranberries and cloudberries, and mushrooms grow all over the place in fall, even right up to our porches. And the woods are gloomy, thick with conifers and clearings that aren't clear at all. Which is why the wildlife – the moose (such a handsome boy), the wild boar, the bear, the wolf, and no telling what-all else – also has a soft spot for the place we call home.

From time immemorial, people have settled along the waterways here. The rivers carried the trade in furs and the flax that is the gold of the North. We had a state farm in Soviet times, and well-off it was too. Its name was Struggle, though, and struggle we did – if not with drought, then with bad harvests. Even so, we lived well enough. Think about it – we had a cow in every yard, a pig in every sty, and lots of little lambs. We planted potatoes and carrots, beets, and cabbage, plenty for the family and some to sell. There were apple, plum, and cherry orchards everywhere. We weren't poor, no indeed. The haymaking in the river floodplains and along the lakeshores was good too: all that succulent, tasty grass! And we planted flax that turned the fields sky-blue when it flowered.

We kept ourselves to ourselves. Our village used to be part of a gentleman's estate. General Kuropatkin, a hero of the Russo-Japanese War of 1904 and 1905 and a progressive thinker, spent his own money to build a post office, a school, and a hospital with a maternity ward. The place teemed with people: the state farm ended up taking over twelve – count 'em, twelve! – well-populated villages. And there were old folks who had lived here forever. One old gal, a hundred and two if

she was a day, said she remembered her grandpa going off to fight against Napoleon. Before the Soviets came, our lands had been in the province of Pskov though later, for some reason, they made them part of Tver Province.

But when perestroika began, it all just fell apart. The state farm hung on like grim death, and it sure was grim at times. Our little village ended up with six houses and four old gals – Vasilyevna, Mikhalna, Nikolavna, and stone-deaf Zinka. There's only one grandpa in the whole place, and that's Vasya, and he's hard of hearing too, but he still plays the accordion. Next door lives my pal Nadyukha – she'll never see fifty again – and her husband, Mishka Sparrowlegs, who used to be a stableman and a welder, but is now unemployed, a dedicated drunk, and a bitter man.

And then there's Sanechka Owlface who pastures the cows, all two of them, and Nikolayev the tractor driver, who's pretty new to the village and lives on the far outskirts with his mother-in-law and his wife, Ninka. We're thin on the ground, you could say, but in summer the seasonal visitors arrive, from Moscow or St. Petersburg, and all of a sudden life's fun again, and noisy too. Come autumn, it all goes quiet. We dig potatoes, get firewood in for the winter, and caulk our huts one more time, so we won't freeze to death.

It's not far to the store as the crow flies, just a mile or so at most, but Boy, a staid and thoughtful horse, is being hitched up for the trip. Mishka Sparrowlegs is fussing in the stable, taking the tack down from the wall, leading Boy out onto the hard-packed, hay-veined snow, and slapping the horse affectionately on the rump. Then he says something in Boy's ear that makes him toss his head and bare his big, yellow teeth.

Mishka has taught him to "laugh" so, to amuse the kiddies, he says, "Boy, gimme a smile." For that the horse gets scraps of moistened cookie or little caramels, held out on tiny palms. He takes the treat neatly, although that lip could easily wrap around the child's whole hand, mitten and all.

Mishka solemnly drags out the hand-made wooden sleigh, checks the harness, plumps up the hay-stuffed cushion, and shakes out a fringed blanket of burgundy velvet that he got for free when the local club had no further use for it.

And now, sensing that he's the center of attention, Boy starts bowing, raising his front leg, and flashing his white socks. He's a sleek horse, well fed and well cared for (Sparrowlegs is half gypsy, so he knows his horseflesh). The manager comes out of the canteen, carrying under his arm a roll of canvas sacks and a black oilskin satchel like a conductor's bag. The old gals, who have been stamping their felt-booted feet in the cold, take this as an "All aboard" and go to find their places in the sleigh.

Mishka sits up front, flourishes his whip in figure eights, tugs on the reins, and gives an encouraging "Giddyup, Boy, giddyup." And Boy jerks the sleigh forward in a grudging sort of way. They labor up the post-office hill, the horse making heavy going of it. Mishka's walking alongside to lighten the load, while the old gals squeal and tilt backward with every jolt.

Boy picks it up on the downhill slope, cutting his eyes sideways, fairly barreling along, and scaring the neighborhood dogs. He sets a chipper pace, his hooves mashing down the snow.

"Oh, great," sighs the crowd in the store, "the hospital's back." They know that these customers have lists as long as your arm and they'll take forever, so the men go off to have a smoke and the women head for the stove, to yap about the latest news. Mishka is back in the sleigh, lying on the hay and smoking a cigarette of his own. The smoke funnels upward, into the cold.

NIKOLAYEV'S BIRTHDAY

It was Nikolayev's birthday, which in ordinary years would always start bright and early, with his best buddies tossing pebbles at his window, hinting that a new life had begun and what did that call for? A celebratory drink, or two, or three, that's what. Nikolayev, embarrassed by his own stinginess, would have been down to the district general store ahead of time and laid his hands on the two prescribed bottles of store-bought vodka and some nondescript snacks like caramel candies or stale cheese with a name like "Kam-am-ber" that was meaningless to the Russian ear. And only after that, their souls cheered by the spectacle of the day breaking to a burst of birdsong, the whole troop would parade off down the main street to the motor pool and tractor depot, to set the tractors up with parts lost during the hard-fought campaign to bring in the harvest.

Toward evening, they'd gather at Nikolayev's hut, where his wife, her mouth smeared with scarlet lipstick, would sling onto the table a pot of oven-boiled new potatoes generously sprinkled with dill, use her apron to wipe off some dusty six-pint jars of pickled tomatoes, going out of her way to pick out the jar with the biggest ones, and fry some summer squash, all green and blimpy. Their daughter would be grating beetroot – also last year's and already putting out young leaves – on Grandma's grater. Mayonnaise rarely showed up in the deliveries to the store, so the dressing would be vegetable oil.

"Put some vinegar in it," the mother-in-law would chip in from behind the curtain that separated the kitchen from the main room. "And add mustard!"

Mother-in-law would be charged with the most momentous job of all, the slicing of the sausage. A brother-in-law, now a head honcho of some kind, would have got hold of the sausage in town just in time for the big day. Ma-in-law, with Grandpa's glasses on for good measure and sticking out her tongue with the strain of it, would cut thin, transparent little circles from the stick of

sausage and lay them in a spiral on the plate. But they'd never be tight-fisted with the lard, which had been kept in the cellar since last year's November holiday.

They would sit down at the table all prim and proper, after the men had had their smoke and the women were done hanging out in the entryway, elbowing each other and preening in front of the dim, speckled shard of mirror tacked up at an angle over the washstand. Guests would drift into the main room, bowing to the holy corner, although there hadn't been any icons there for ages. The neighbor women, their chubby shoulders bundled in colorful triangle shawls, would survey the table and scour the room with their eyes, checking it out for something new: curtains, an armoire maybe, a chandelier? The men made little throat-clearing noises as they guesstimated how much vodka was on the table and figured out how much should still be stored up in the cellar, given the number of folks who were there.

The first toast to the birth-day boy wasn't going to happen, though, not until everyone was served with a piece of bread. The mother-in-law would have baked a big, fancy loaf, because nobody else knew how to get bread to rise so high and look so gorgeous. Although ma-in-law was generally hazardous to other life forms, she did have a way with dough. Well, and so it wasn't until chunks were bro-ken off the loaf that they started on the drinking, then the danc-ing, then, when the dancing was over, the fighting – amiably, though, and cheerfully, and always following the rule that bans any flailing of fists indoors.

Once the guests left, the wife and mother-in-law would tally up the presents (trinkets, all of them) before separating out the leftovers for the pigs and washing the plates with mustard powder in a big bowl full of steaming water. Nikolayev, the happy man, would be lying on the conjugal bed with his arms flung out, still in his jacket, giving a rousing rendition of "The International" through his nose.

That, now, was a proper birthday, as much a collective effort as Soviet power itself. But this time, something incomprehensible had happened. On that day of days, Nikolayev was left on his lonesome. And it was all because of the mother-in-law, enemy of the human race! She'd taken it into her head to haul her sizable self up onto a stool so she could take the curtains down to be washed, and what stool leg could put up with that? The leg gave way, the old gal came crashing down with a howl, and they carted her off to the district hospital, still clutching a curtain. Of course, the wife and kids went along in the ambulance, because when would there be another chance to get some shopping done in town?

Nikolayev, in his best jacket, ambled around the messy hut. The July darkness was seeping through the uncurtained windows and crawling about every which way. Nikolayev was suffocating on his tears. But Russian men are real men, and they never surrender! So Nikolayev strode boldly to the hutch cupboard. A huge length of white fabric went on the table, with Nikolayev straightening it out nice and neat all the way around, after deciding that this tablecloth was just what the occasion called for. The stamp that read "Rgnl. Hospital No. 5" had puzzled him, but not for long. After a bit of banging and crashing in the china closet, Nikolayev tracked down a complete set of dinnerware with gilded rims and worn roses on the flat part of the plates. He wiped the pressed-crystal shot glasses with the tablecloth, lined them up by height, and for some unknown reason added a couple of blue-glass tumblers. He was going for four covers – four table settings, that is. He'd heard the word "covers" once in a TV serial about the Empress Catherine, found it inspiring, and committed it to memory. The silverware was wobbly on the table. But Nikolayev cushioned each set with cheery little napkins left over from Easter that had chicks on them.

Now to the main event. The pot with its pinkish potatoes had been sitting in the oven for ages, and a can of meat stew was turned loose into a cast-iron frying pan. Nikolayev didn't go all the way down into the cellar, instead just leaning in and groping around until he found a jar of pickled cucumbers sealed with a plastic cap. Then he couldn't help himself; he opened it on the spot and shamefacedly ate the biggest one, which was entangled in dill fronds and mantled in horseradish leaves. Next came the milk cap mushrooms, brined in a lidded enamel bucket. Nikolayev scooped them out with his hand into a glass salad bowl. After a little thought, he also grabbed a jar of cherry juice and, again for some unknown reason, a store-bought can of sprats. Last year's pickled cabbage was out in the entryway. The wife had put it out there as piglet feed, but Nikolayev had forgotten about it. He dumped a whole lot of it into a soup tureen. He laid slices of Antonov apples, stained red from the cranberries, in a circle. Then, foraging around like a wolf in a henhouse, Nikolayev collected yet more food to put on the well-stocked table, even bringing a rusty can of cod's liver, some green peas, and two cartons of ramen noodles into the act. The vodka was no problem, because Nikolayev had his home brew stashed everywhere. There were bottles of the unforgiving cinquefoil vodka, of rowanberry vodka, horseradish vodka, and nettle vodka in the workshop, while the mild, girly varieties – the cranberry vodka, wild currant vodka, and suchlike – were crammed into every corner of the hut.

Nikolayev gave his hands a ceremonial wash with a clatter of the washstand nozzle, doused his neck with his wife's perfume, and, wiping his hands, sat down at the table.

Pouring himself a nip of cinquefoil vodka into a shot glass, he filled a tumbler with the cherry juice, rose to his feet, solemnly declared, "Happy birthday to you, my dear man!" and knocked it back. Then he sat down, deflated. The bread! He'd forgotten to buy bread, and there was no big, fancy loaf. His birthday had been hopelessly ruined.

THE HEAT

There's no doing without hay in the village. The cows eat it, and the sheep, and the hens need loads of it for their nests. And it comes in handy for people too, when they stuff their mattresses with it and lie on them forevermore, because the scent is just so marvelous.

The collective farm is serious about hay-making. There's tractors for that, and all sorts of technical stuff. But the smallholders are on their own. So they muster a few people together and are hauled to a hay meadow far away and off limits to any tractor.

They mow by hand, old school, with a scythe. And what's a scythe? A wooden handle with a blade on the end (they call it a *litovka* around here). You have to have the knack of it, and the scythe has to fit you just right, the handle not too long or too short. The mowers always work in a staggered line, one behind the other, so you won't poke your neighbor with the sharp end.

Mowing's always the most bothersome time in the village. You can't let so much as a day slip by, else you'll be mowing when the rain comes down and the hay's ruined. So in the sunny weather, the folk come together at four in the morning while the dew's still on the grass. Because that's the time for mowing. You work until noon, and by then you're so roasted, you'd do anything to crawl to the nearest stream and dunk your head in it, so hot it is. Black flies and horseflies and mosquitoes eat you alive, and you can run faster than the wind but they'll still catch up with you. Or you can lie in a patch of shade with your head covered, but when the sun moves, so must you.

In the towns they eat ice cream and drink beer, but for us in the village, it's kvas and birch juice. In big canisters that are put into a stream, and it doesn't get any better than that. Especially when you're lounging on the hay.

But once the mown hay starts drying, it's time to turn it. So here come the gals again. They go in a line too, with their rakes, stirring the hay so it'll dry all the way. Someone will come along later with pitchforks, to pile it up. And if that isn't the hardest part! The horseflies are biting, you're sweating buckets, three yards feels like a thousand.

Now the hay's in piles, and the mowers sit in the shade, get ahold of some kvas or some milk with a frog in it, sit themselves down, and take a break.[1] The gals are dressed every which way, some in frocks, some in jogging pants, and the young 'uns are stripped right down to their lacy underwear. The main thing, though, is to keep your head from baking.

Men are in short supply, so there's just Vaska the stable hand, squint-eyed old Sashka, and our livestock specialist, who's been named Ivanych the Uzbek.

Melya's lying at the foot of a hay pile, with her legs stretched out. "Oh, I don't like the heat, not one bit," she says. "I don't even go to the banya in summertime. My mama taught me that when it's hot, you take a white hen, feed her some soaked peas and, and put her on your head."

"If that isn't the stupidest thing! Isn't the hen hot too?"

"But what if you've slit her throat first, eh?" Melya's trying to remember it right. "And what if it's not a chicken? What if you eat the peas yourself?"

"Ah... She was talking about a pillow. If you fill a pillow with white chicken feathers, you need to put that on your head, to keep it from baking." Vita has covered her face with her headscarf. "I get so toasty in the sun, I turn into a stove. Put a teakettle on me" – she slaps herself on the belly – "and it'll boil, eh?"

---

1. No kidding. Frogs are supposed to keep milk drinkable for longer because of the antibacterial properties of their skin: bit.ly/frogs-in-milk

"I'm cold in Russia," says Ivanych the Uzbek. "I love it in Fergana, sit in a tearoom, eat pilaf, drink tea, so good. Hot! And good! Cotton's good in the heat. And the pilaf's lovely, rich, with lamb in it."

"Oh, I couldn't swallow a bite." Ninka fishes the frog out of the jar and puts it on the ground. Blinking angrily, the milk-drenched frog hops to one side, where it is promptly eaten by one of the storks that hang around here in mowing season. "All I can do is drink."

Vita bites into a boiled egg. "You drink plenty when it's cold too," she says. "But I eat when I'm hungry. You shameless hussy, you could at least put on a smock. Running around in your undies and riling up the menfolk!"

"At least their pitchforks are nice and straight," Ninka sasses back, straightening her lacy shoulder strap. "Why swelter, anyway? And you get a better tan when it's hot like this. Let 'em think we're down by the sea…"

Ivanych the Uzbek pours tea from a thermos into a bowl. "At home in Fergana, women can't never be bare-naked," he says. "We be strict with our women. I ain't standing for no woman without a veil. They only go naked in the banya."

"Yes, but your women wander about in sacks." Melya says, pulling a well-laundered towel out of her basket. "Vaska! Go down to the stream and wet this rag for a girl, won't you?" Vaska, who's dozing in a scrap of shade, turns his back. "They put on sacks and go about dripping with sweat. I saw a movie at the club. About the sun in the desert. Just awful."

She heaves herself up and goes to the stream, but it's run dry. So instead she dampens the rag with the murky water in the big can and wipes herself off. Turns around to see if anyone's looking. And scoops up water to splash herself.

"I love eat baklava too," says Ivanych the Uzbek. "Love meat and noodles, that's *beshbarmak*. No vodka, though." But while he's talking, Vaska, the sometime tractor driver, is pouring vodka into his tea on the sly. "Oh, tea, tea! Tasty tea!" Ivanych goes on. "Bad to drink vodka, good to drink tea!"

Squint-eyed Sashka wipes his damp forehead with his cap. "Aren't you sweating in your robe, Ivanych?" he asks. "Isn't it like if I was to go mowing in a quilted jacket?"

"Their robes work like thermoses," Zoya explains (she's a schoolteacher). "The body stays at the same temperature. But Ninka's naked, and she'll get sunstroke. And then peel like a shedding cat. Enough chitchat now. On your feet!"

Reluctantly, the gals get up and figure out whose rake is whose, while the men get ahold of their pitchforks. Vaska brings up the horse-drawn cart, and the work goes full swing again.

An inky-black cloud is swelling on the horizon. The gals go faster and faster across the field, stacking the hay into ricks without even looking, just to get finished before the rain.

When the first fat drops fall, leaving spots on their clothing, the gals clamber into the cart, old Sashka jumps up front with Vaska, and the horse plods off toward the village.

They all get down at the collective farm office, but that's when Melya throws up her hands.

"Lordy lord! Where's our Uzbek? Where's Ivanych? How are we going to report this? Where's he gotten to? Oh rats, our livestock specialist's gone missing!"

"Hey, guys, and where's Ninka? Where's naked Ninka? Struck by lightning, d'you think?"

They're all standing in the rain, looking at each other. Well, of course: if people are lost, they need to be found. But who wants to go out in a storm? One lightning strike, and you're a goner.

They trail into the office, to sit and wait out the storm. Toward evening, everything quietens down. The gals are sent home, except for the teacher, who heads back to the hayfield with the stable boy. And they start walking around and hallooing.

"Ivanych the Uzbek! Ninka! Halloo! Where are you! Are you alive?"

No one. Silence. It smells of new-mown hay and horse manure.

"They must have run into the woods," Vaska says hopefully. So off they go, to yell in the bushes. Silence. And not until it's completely dark, when they decide to comb the field one more time, do they hear the snores coming from beneath a rick. They pull it apart, and there's our Ivanych the Uzbek fast asleep, hugging his thermos and smacking his lips. They shake him.

"Oh, such tasty tea! Oh, such strong tea! I had a dream, slept so hard."

"Uh-huh. It's hot in a rick, just like in a robe, right?"

Laughing, they rummage around in the other side of the rick, and there's the sleeping Ninka, curled into a ball.

"Ninka!"

"Oh!" She's waking up. She's got hay in her hair. "Where am I?"

"Must be way down south, in Fergana," they laugh. "Why'd you crawl into the rick?"

"I was freezing cold," she tells them. "And it's warm in the rick, just..."

Vaska has to have the last word. "Just like in a nice, snug robe?" he asks.

KVAS

Our old gals in the village cast a wary eye on all food from the store, because who knows what they've got in there? Homemade, that's the only way to go. And that is why even now they bake their own bread, and brew their own moonshine, and when it comes to kvas, that refreshing black-bread beer, why waste the money? Granny Melya's grandma taught her to brew kvas and here's Melya teaching her granddaughter, Anka. Anka's city folk, but she knows how to respect the homespun recipes. The experience of centuries, she calls them. No chemicals. Microelements. Vitamins. A healthy lifestyle. So Granny lies on the stove bench, warming herself, and bosses Anka around: "Fetch water from the spring," she says. "Strip leaves off the young currant branches. And the hop cones are back there, in a sack hanging in the storeroom."

"How about raisins, Granny?"

"What raisins? Raisins don't grow here."

But Anka isn't about to let this go. "Then what's going to ferment it?" she wants to know.

"Get the dough starter. It's in a jug on the porch, under the bench. Did you buy the bread?"

"I did, I did."

Anka slices chunks of crust off the rye loaf and dries them in the stove until they're as black as coal, to make the kvas good and dark. The real thing.

She heats the spring water in a pot so huge she could crawl right into it. Her drowsy-eyed granny is yelling at her from the stove.

"Don't pour the sugar into the boiling water. Let it cool."

Anka dips her little finger in, to test how hot it is, then starts "mixing" the kvas. (That's the word they use around here.) She pours in the starter, scatters the slices that smell of burnt bread on top, and, with a quick sideways glance in her granny's general direction, dumps in some city-bought raisins. The pot starts a merry hissing and burbling; it's come alive. Now the mash needs to be strained through a cloth into bottles that are securely stoppered and whisked away into the cold, to "finish off."

There are no glass bottles to be had for love or money, only plastic ones, and that sets Granny off: "Ugh, nasty! Don't pour it into those all-be-damned chemical doo-dads! How many glass bottles get tossed out behind the store? We'll give 'em a quick wash and be done."

With a deeply meaningful clearing of the throat, Anka pours the kvas mash, spreading a satisfying smell of bread through the hut. Yawning, she stuffs the black-currant leaves into the bottles, along with shaved horseradish, the fragrant hop cones, and, secretly, some lemon rinds, because there's no accounting for taste, as Granny Melya says.

Half the bottles are crammed into the door of the imported fridge that Granny got as a name-day gift. Those that won't fit, Anka takes down into the cellar.

It's all done, and, downing a glass of moonshine for good luck, she tumbles into bed.

The following day, a storm came crashing down on the village. Thunder, lightning, the lights promptly went out, and grandmother and granddaughter sat for three days playing cards and trading gossip.

"In the war, time was when they'd up and start bombing, and that was that. Boom! Bang! Your ears get all clogged, and it's so scary. So I'd creep into the cellar. I'd take the cat, a book, a candle… You can't play a club, hearts are trumps!" Granny swats at Anka with her cards because the war stories have been putting her to sleep.

That night Anka felt one heck of a jolt. The explosion was strong enough to deafen her.

"This is it," she thought. "It's started."

She went groping around for a candle, all the while wondering why there was water on the floor, ankle deep. The water was warm and oddly fizzy. Then the light came on all by itself, and Anka gasped in dismay.

The fridge door had been ripped off its hinges and was twisted into a figure eight. The kvas bottles had exploded from being kept in a warm fridge and were spinning across the floor like pinwheels in a fireworks display. Everything was dripping with sweet, sticky kvas. The raisins had made a monogram-like pattern on the ceiling, and the lemon rinds had glued themselves to the curtains like gumdrops, making the old

tulle glint and glimmer. Granddad's portrait was festooned with currant leaves, and the horseradish shavings were floating about like wood chips.

Granny, horrorstruck, tumbled off the stove but did it well, landing in the basket where the cat slept. The cat, meanwhile, was wandering through the goopy mess, squeamishly shaking her paws off with every step.

They spent the whole next day washing the hut, laundering the curtains, and whitewashing the ceiling. Fortunately there was still the kvas in the cellar, but nobody even wanted to drink it, so sorry they were for the poor, blown-out refrigerator.

The next day it turned really hot. Anka and her Granny were butts-up in the vegetable patch, glancing from time to time at the dusty road and the people walking along it. The way it worked out, though, those people were walking with their heads downward and their feet sticking up.

All at once, Granny and Anka saw a huge black spool rolling across the sky. It was wound with threads,
like, but thick ones.
And there were guys
wandering along
with it. Granny and
granddaughter tore
themselves away from
the vegetable rows, and the
world turned right side up again.
The people walking – the guys, that is – were glum
and dusty-gray, and they were rolling the spool ahead of them.

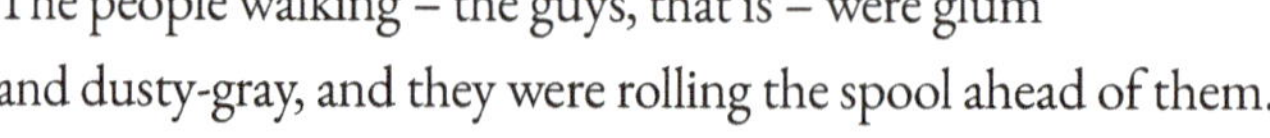

"Hey, lads," Granny yells. "What's that? What're you going to stitch?"

They laugh.

"We're going to stitch you to the telephone, old girl. You'll be calling your kids in town."

Pleased as can be, Granny starts bustling about.

"Come take a seat, my darlings," she says. "Rest up in the shade under the awning on the porch here."

And when did any guy ever turn down the chance to take a load off? They sat down, stripped off their shirts, fired up their smokes; they'd been working their tails off. The spool sat out there in the sun, its cable reeking of chemicals.

"Get us a drink, lady," the head guy says. "We're done in, what with the heat and these hard roads."

"In a jiffy, my dearies."

And Granny scurries into the hut, telling Anka, "Out you go. There's some fine-looking marriage material out there."

Anka shows herself, sleek as a swan.

"Well now, you hardworking fellows," she says. "Shall I fetch you some nice cold kvas?"

And she winks at her Granny.

"Fetch it, do, if it's not too much trouble, my beauty." The second guy smiles, pocks and freckles and all.

So Anka brought out Granny's baking pan, lined it with newspaper, put a pretty towel on top, and got mugs from the china cabinet. Crisp little poppy-seed bread rings went onto a plate, along with pickled cucumber for no particular reason. She dove down into the cellar and came up with a bottle of kvas, beaded with moisture and looking just like cola, but even better. And she carried it all out onto the porch, a princess to the life.

The lads are actually squinting, so lovely is the relief they're feeling. They down a mug apiece, then another.

Anka sails off again, swan-like, and brings another bottle to uncork. The guys drink and say good things about what they're drinking. But the words start coming out slurred.

"Da-a-a-amn," the second-in-command blurts out. "Did you buy this kvas, Ma? Is it a store brand?"

"Don't insult me like that, good fellows. It's as homebrewed as they come."

"That's it," the head guy says, slamming his cap down into the dust. "Wrap it up. To hell with the work. We've worked enough. For shame, Ma – we was all on the wagon. Been in treatment since May first. But this ain't no kvas. It's the hard stuff."

"That wasn't on purpose," Anka says, fussing and flapping. "Forgive us, good fellows, you hardworking fellows!"

They left the reel where it was and off they went, as if they'd never been there at all. Homemade kvas always has a kick to it. And if it's given extra fermenting time, that makes it better than any champagne.

THE POST OFFICE

The only things in the village more important than the post office are the store that sells bread and the walk-in clinic. But when you come right down to it, the post office really is the bigger deal. The master built it back in the day, to use as a school, so it's solid and roomy, and has little stoves to keep things toasty. And so very orderly it is, with a separate office for the savings bank, and a room for outgoing packages, and even a special place to hand in newspaper subscriptions. The main room is where the post and telegraph clerks sit, behind a counter covered with blue linoleum and painted a reddish brown.

Postmaster Ilya Semyonovich Yablochkin is a bulky bulldog of a man. He wears a skull-cap to hide his bald spot, and sateen sleevelets to hide the fact that his shirt is out at the elbows. Yablochkin knows his worth and his customers' too, which is why he torments them, making them wait in line until they are good and docile. He moves the abacus beads slowly back and forth to tally things up, writes even more slowly to fill out forms and registers, and, with regal dignity, takes out the book that has a pocket to hold stamps, and extracts them with licked fingers. He loves illustrated envelopes, and better yet if the picture celebrates the current date. He only accepts packages that are neatly sewn up in white fabric inscribed legibly, with the who to, the where to, and the who from. The sender gets confused, scampers off to rewrite the form, and messes up for the hundredth time (it's so hard not to put the amount in numbers), while the entire line is hissing and yelling mean things, because everyone knows that the same fate is awaiting them. The grand finale is the stamping of the outgoing mail, for which purpose a little pan of sealing wax is kept boiling on a small electric hot plate. With the deep sigh appropriate to the guardian of a state secret, Yablochkin stands up and takes a special wooden-handled seal from the safe. Dripping the wax onto wherever string meets string, he presses the seal down with great deliberation, then lifts it and admires his handiwork.

ВНИМАНИЕ

Ninka the telephone lady sits at a separate counter, mumbling "Town exchange, town exchange, hey girls, Sheshurino calling, come in... Town exchange, town exchange..." into her mouthpiece. It's as if she's chewing on the words. The line is always busy. The wooden benches are occupied by biddies with children, business travelers, casual laborers here to build a cow barn, and suchlike nobodies. And all of a sudden, Ninka yells "Kherson? Booth two. Move it, move it! Who wants Kherson? Fifteen minutes!" A little man darts across the room, dropping his briefcase on the way, and starts yelling so the whole post office can hear, "Masha? Masha! I'm stuck here for two days! Masha! We're being audited!" At which every single person there smirks, because they all know that the old pops from Kherson has hooked up with Valka the shop girl and has been wearing himself out with her in the sweltering heat, on a stove bench padded with feather-filled coverlets.

The mail carriers are supervised by the deputy postmistress, the chunky, blue-housecoat-wearing, lackadaisical Valentina. She rakes her pencil right through the subscription form, tearing it and crossing out everything except the district newspaper. 'Na-taaa-sha," she says in her singsong way, "you know very well there's limits on everything. You want a sub for *Rural Life*, starting in January? But... you know that's not happening. No *Peasant Woman* neither. *Working Woman*, nope. *Pioneer*, nope. And what d'you want with the

latest fashions? That's what the library's for." And that's the extent of her sympathy for schoolteacher Natasha. Meanwhile, Valentina's taking out subscriptions to hard-to-find magazines for her girlfriends and all the right people. Meaning that she's making good use of her official position.

At a round table covered with linoleum patterned to look like marble, an old gal from a faraway village sits. Puddles have spread all around her overshoes, and she's hot from the stove that gobbles up wrapping paper and spoiled forms. She slips a gray goat-down shawl onto her shoulders, unties a cotton scarf, white with blue specks, and uses it to mop her forehead. Fumbling in her oilskin bag, faintly berating herself for the old fool and blockhead that she is, she finds her spectacles and, holding them like a magnifying glass, starts scrawling text for a telegram, skittering the pen across the paper, making star-shaped blots, and quietly agonizing over the weakness of her eyes and the feebleness of her brain. She calls over a young whippersnapper who's capering around alongside his mama, proud recipient of a money transfer from the city, and asks him for help, so the kid dashes off, in big skewed letters, "doter cumme grannies sick will dye if you don't." With a sigh of relief, the old girl heaves herself up and takes her place at the end of the line.

Over the entrance to the savings bank, which occupies a corner office just off the main room, hangs a poster showing a pink-cheeked young man buying savings bonds. He's flashing a snowy-toothed smile and pointing with a clean, pink hand at a house, a car, and a beautiful wife in an imported fur coat. The old lady peers into her money purse, which is sewn up on one side with a thick black thread, and heaves a rueful sigh. On all the walls, overlapping like the scales on a fish, are directives, orders, examples of completed forms, and other such bureaucratic folderol that no one ever reads.

Lunch time's creeping closer, and Yablochkin is already groping for the sign that reads, in no uncertain terms, "LUNCH," when workers from the logging company come barreling in, filling up the whole place. They've just been paid, so now they're going to be sending remittances home. Shading his eyes with one hand, like the captain of a ship, Yablochkin watches to make sure they don't walk off with the inkwell. Or any pencils. Or draw moustaches on Lenin's portrait. Or write four-letter words anywhere. They smell of diesel fuel, tar, and cheap tobacco, and they're swarming all over the little tables, while their foreman, biting his lips, writes addresses on the forms.

Then the door crashes open, nearly shaking the spring loose in the process, and in swoops a little woman, limping on her left leg. It's Nadka Rukomylo, a nasty, drunken troublemaker. Her coat is flapping open, her headscarf has come untied, and Nadka means business. She pummels the foreman for all she's worth with her oilskin bag, which ends in him blotting a form and punching her in the eye with his free hand. Yablochkin blows a whistle he keeps stashed away for spats like these, and the combatants are dragged to separate sides of the room. The foreman, who owes Nadka for the corner he's renting in her home, counts out the rubles and sprinkles a hillock of coins on top, with a look that says, "Here, choke on it."

It's now exactly five minutes to lunchtime, so Yablochkin, emerging from behind the counter, pulls on his sheepskin jacket and fur overcoat, and in a combat veteran's far-from-indoor voice, roars, "LUNCH!"

And everyone obediently files out of the post office, and for a whole hour, while the padlock sits on the door collecting frost, they crowd together, stamping their chilly feet, smoking, and cussing Nadka, who's to blame for them having to spend the next sixty minutes out there in the freezing cold.

A STOVE NAMED YEROFEYICH

Auntie Nina stood in the middle of her hut and wept. The place once occupied by the Russian stove built back in her grandma's day, in the 1930s, the place where that unfailing dispenser of tender loving care used to stand, was empty. A ragged hole yawned in the ceiling above, giving a clear view of a mournful sky and the white caterpillar of an airplane vapor trail. Auntie Nina even pinched herself in the side, but no – it wasn't a dream.

Grandpa Yerofeyich had built that stove, so the family lovingly called it Yerofeyich too. And why not, because what's most important of all in a Russian village? The stove, sure enough. In times past, after the war, only the stoves loomed like solitary monuments in the burned-out villages. The huts were rebuilt around them, and life began anew.

Auntie Nina remembered her grandmother's saying, that the Russian stove was the empress of the home. It warmed the whole huge hut, giving out a steady, welcoming heat, and everyone – Grandpa, Grandma, Ma and Pa, and the little ones too – would crowd around it, rubbing their hands. Grandma would sleep on the stove's high wooden shelf, while the kiddies monkeyed around on the floor, and Mom put a cast-iron pot of kasha and milk onto the stove to stew, and deep in its enormous, ship-like innards, the stuffed pies baked, and you could see the dough rising and the plate pies browning before your eyes. And as night fell, the coals were raked, and the children sat and watched, and to them it seemed that they were peering into the sky and the bright little embers were stars.

Auntie Nina wiped her eyes. For a long time the stove had been smoking and sneezing, and its flanks were no longer giving off heat. She'd been urged to bring in one of those new-fangled stove repairmen to clean the flue and the pipes, replace the crumbling tiles, and fix the whole thing up.

So Papanin, a burly fellow with fists the size of footballs, appeared, asked for payment in advance, rustled up some buddies, and sent Auntie Nina off to stay with her sister on the outskirts of the village, so she wouldn't get in the way. Nina left with a light heart, although she did take with her the satchel that held her cash and documents.

A week later, she came back. And gasped in dismay. The hut was full of smoke, it reeked of kerosene and exhaust fumes, and there, in the middle of it all, Papanin slept, his arms folded across his chest. "He's kicked the bucket!" Nina moaned, and dashed off to fetch the medic. But when she came back with the medic in tow, Papanin and the canister of home-brewed beer were long gone. There was nothing left of Yerofeyich either, except the foundation and a pile of broken bricks.

Auntie Nina slumped onto a stool and bawled her head off. It would be turning cold soon enough, and how could anyone get through the winter without a stove? The seasonal visitors from town were putting in fancy water heaters and radiators because they looked nicer, but where was the sense in that? The village electricity supply was always here today, gone tomorrow, but a stove doesn't need electricity to work. It runs all on its own, warming place and people, and even gives light when light's needed.

And what about cooking? Auntie Nina sobbed some more. Where were the cast-iron pots supposed to go? Cooking with gas was expensive, and the food just didn't taste right. What about baking milk? And drying socks? And felt boots? And what's a girl to do with the sack of dried birch leaves? And how's she going to warm the small of her back? On a radiator? Oh, what a disaster! Whatever fun is to be had indoors, it's all because of the stove. Every proverb is about the stove, the dear and darling stove. Auntie Nina picked up a mat soiled by Papanin's great clodhopping feet and went outside to beat it.

And she heard someone cough behind the fence. She looked, and there was a little man wearing a cap and carrying a bag.

"Who are you?" she wanted to know.

"I build stoves," the little man replied. "Would you happen to need one installed, my dear lady? You can call me Fedka."

"Do you drink?" Nina brandished a rolling pin and started thrashing the striped rug that she'd draped over the wattle fence. "Hear me? Do you drink?"

"In what way?" Fedka asked coyly, breathing into his cupped palm and bringing it back up to his nose. Booze breath, for sure, but hardly noticeable.

"What d'you mean, in what way? In the Russian way!" Auntie Nina was pounding so hard with the rolling pin that the fence-post cracked. "In the way that the lot of you drink, you Herods of Judea."

"I, madam," said Fedka, truckling just enough to disgust even himself, "drink only on public holidays. Like New Year's, Easter, and such ... and Women's Day. And what of it?"

Nina wiped her forehead with her house coat hem. "This is what," she said. "You'll spend at least a week building it, and you'll never touch a drop, else I won't pay your bill. Now tell me what you need to get the job done."

Fedka shuffled his feet, shrugged his backpack strap off his shoulder, and struck a dignified pose.

"You, my dear lady, don't pussyfoot around. No, you make straight for the target, like Marshal Budyonny, and we're the White troops that he fought and beat. Except that fear has no place in this business of ours."

With a sigh, Auntie Nina kicked her outside shoes off at the door and went in with nothing on her feet but gray, hand-knitted socks. Fedka plucked up his courage to follow. He wanted to slip by still wearing his shabby boots, but he was stopped short.

"Off with 'em!"

"To make it more awkward to do my job? How'll I manage, going back and forth?" He waved his arms right and left to show how he'd be here, there, and everywhere. "I won't have the time to be putting them on and taking them off."

"I'll lay some sacking down. What a windbag you are."

Fedka stood in the middle of the room, eyed the holes in the floor and the ceiling, seemed to run his fingers over an invisible wall, and asked in an unexpectedly intimidating tone, "Where are we putting the stoking hole? What are the specifications for the sleeping ledge, how many interior channels do you want, what dimensions do I have to ponder?"

And Fedka gave Auntie Nina a menacing look.

No longer armed with her rolling pin, Nina was a whole lot less fiery. Instead, now she'd grasped the true scope of the work, she was back to her moaning and groaning.

"Oh, Fyodor Mikhalych, work with me, do! I want our stove, a Russian stove, a stove like my grandma had. Yes?"

"With an arched opening?" Fedka gasped. Until that very moment, he'd been hoping this would be a piece of cake. "An arch! That'll cost money, big money. I've been told it'd be an ordinary stove with a straightforward baffle system, and then along comes milady with a task like this. Who builds a Russian stove that way anymore? Buy a gas stove, why don't you? What're you going to do for bricks?"

"Use the bricks from before, from before."

"Reclaimed ones, you mean," Fedka said, bringing the debate to a screeching halt. "So they've to be cleaned up. And who knows where the clay's to come from? And the sand with pebbles in it? And the only help I'll have is you, old girl. And to top it all off, 'No drinking, no drinking,'" he taunted, maliciously mimicking his new client. "You try building a stove under conditions like that."

"Have pity!" Nina collapsed to the floor, but not to crouch at the stove builder's feet in humble supplication. Rather, she seemed to have been poleaxed by disbelief at the likely cost. "Do it! How can I live without a stove? See, that Herod of Judea, that odd-job man, that swindler if ever there was one, see what a mess he's made! And as if that wasn't enough, he's made off with the cast-iron pots and the milk cans. Help an old lady!" Nina shot a look at Fedka, and Fedka visibly softened. "And you'll have a nip of something now, long and far as you've traveled. Won't you, dearie?"

"No!" Fedka said proudly, rolling the bitter saliva around in his mouth. "When we've got the job done, that's when we'll wet our whistles. Take me to the bricks, so I can see if they're good for anything. And then off you go, my old girl, and find me some horse manure wherever you will, and some coarse salt, rock salt."

Auntie Nina's jaw fell. "But what d'you want manure for? And why horse manure? Where'm I going to find a horse? There's a cow, and that's all there is."

"To seal the seams. Cow manure's not one bit of good. Too sloppy. But a horse makes nice, dry manure, and the hay in it is as good as it gets. Like for when you're installing the facing, and the hay burns off in the heat, so the cladding takes hold just as tight as them Dutch tiles ever could."

Stepping out over the threshold, Fedka crammed his feet into his boots, squashing the backs down. Then he glared at Auntie Nina, made an unexplainably threatening gesture at the gray sky, and strode off toward the barns. And behind him, scampering in figures of eight, came Nina.

Once stern and unbending, out of nowhere she'd become all meek and docile, daunted by the presence of this true craftsman. A Russian stove? No laughing matter, no indeed! And to mark this solemn occasion as it deserved, there'd surely be no harm, after all, in raising a glass or two.

THE TANKMAN AND THE SAILOR

The village of Myakishino had handed all its men over to the war, not that anyone asked their opinion on the matter. In the cemetery, by the ruined church, lay soldiers from other places who'd been brought to the little local hospital. But only two of their own came back, the Tankman and the Sailor – both Sashas and both with the same family name, Smirnov. The Sailor had fought at sea, on a torpedo boat, but he'd got hit just as they were tying up the ship in Murmansk, during Operation Silver Fox, deep in the fall of 1941. After that he rattled around from rear area to rear area and infirmary to infirmary, but then again, Sasha the Sailor was not especially keen on getting back to the front.

He being a two-fisted drinker, as soon as his pension came in, its fate was sealed. He'd be down at the store throwing his money around on drinks for everyone, but then he'd insist they sing with him, and it was always that golden oldie "The Boundless Expanse of the Ocean." But how could you disrespect a combat veteran? So sing they did.

The Sailor was married – to a woman from "way up North," as he put it. Either Finnish or Latvian she was – a spry, dried-up, shrill old thing. They kept rabbits for sale, and the whole village said that the Sailor must know magic spells because for him they bred like mad. So the Sailor would make the rounds, would humbly ask the villagers to let him mow their land, and afterward, he'd shuffle off, stooping under the weight of the grass bundle and roaring "Brave and scrappy were we lads on our torpedo boats..." at the top of his voice.

Back home, his wife from the North would pummel him, and then the Sailor would go to his rabbits and complain to them how he, a combat veteran, a sailor, was being insulted by some German pain-in-the-neck. The Sailor drank home brew straight from the bottle, and the rabbits would wiggle their sensitive pink noses and sneeze.

The other old-timer, Sasha the Tankman, was short-statured (as a tankman should be), thickset, and dour. He'd gone all the way to Vienna in his tank, where he was accidentally put out of action by friendly fire. He was burned but survived, and for the rest of his life had a scorched face, pink as a baby's and browless. That's when he went gray, they said. Though he'd been burned all over, his hair grew back gray, even bluish gray, and yellowish-white. They said all sorts of things about the Tankman, and he wasn't popular in the village. They called him a gray-haired devil and a wood goblin.

The Tankman drank alone, which the village found unforgiveable. He lived on the very outskirts, where the forest came right up on the village and stopped short, as if musing on something. His was a carefree bachelor's life. He kept no livestock, worked as an engineer for the forestry service, made money hand over fist, owned a motorbike and an aluminum boat with an outboard motor, and that's how he lived – pretty much all for show. The ladies loved the Tankman, especially the soldiers' wives, the widows, and they'd visit him in the dark of night, and in plain view, during the day. He'd treat them to sweet wine and spice cookies and, people said, he didn't scrimp on other gifts either, but he outright refused to get married and instead broke things clean off when the hints started, so they wouldn't try it on with him again.

Tongues wagged about his earlier life, to the effect that he'd come home from the war and walked in on his wife in bed with the local police officer, and didn't want to

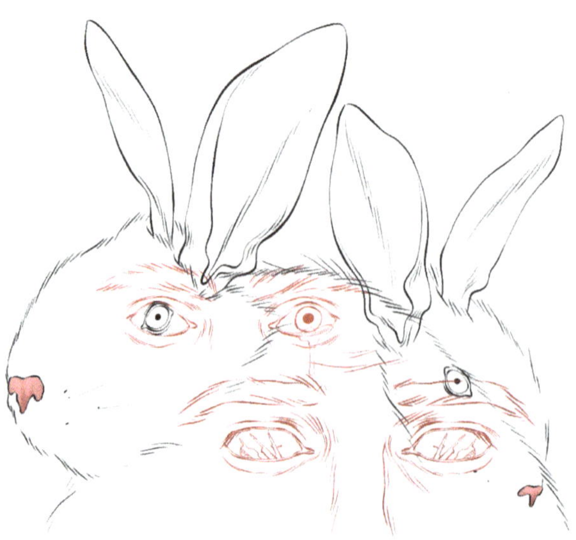

hear a thing about it, so exactly as he'd come, kitbag and all, he took off. Just unloaded his rations onto the table and took off. And his only child, a little boy, blew himself up playing with live munitions – whose they were, no one ever found out, maybe the Germans had mined the place or maybe it was our own Soviet troops. There was fighting everywhere.

The Tankman was friends with nobody but a cat black as soot. Its name was Dirtbag, and it was ferocious. It'd brawl nearly to the death with the neighboring cats and, though it lived in the old man's home, it deigned only to take an occasional saucer of milk there. The Tankman would talk to Dirtbag as if it were a person; the womenfolk would hear him through the fence. It even went fishing with him, sitting on the prow of the boat and meowing.

Once in a while they'd meet up, the Tankman and the Sailor, at haymaking time or when they were helping each other plant potatoes. And they'd talk about everyday things, about how the weather was worse than useless these days, how the hay'd gotten soaked but the clear-cut part of the far forest had caught fire, and how the store had been short on booze again. Never a word about the war. They wouldn't even go to the social club if the movie being shown was about the war. They're all the same, they said, a bunch of malarkey.

There was one time when they did get into it like nobody's business. The Sailor, who'd been out on a bender, was walking along and singing. The Tankman wanted to give him a ride home on his motorbike, and he kind of joked that the Sailor was a seaman, yes, but there he was on foot, just like any old infantryman, while us tankmen ride along, cooler than cool: "Our armor's strong and our tanks are the fastest," as the old song had it. Then the Sailor came back with, "You couldn't even call it fighting, if you weren't at sea." Then the Tankman came back with, "You're a lot of nothing, didn't even serve a year. You've never smelled powder. 'Sailing, sailing, over the ocean blue,' that's what you did. But me, I went all the way to Vienna, and I've got decorations to prove it!" Then the Sailor went, "So show them if you're not just running your mouth." The Tankman saw red. "You don't believe me? Who d'you think you are? I was burned all over. You can see straight off, and never mind the ribbons and bars, what kind of a hero I am." And the Sailor, who wore a mariner's striped shirt until the day he died, ripped his shirt open: "Here, get an eyeful of my decorations." The Tankman looked, and there wasn't a smooth spot to be seen. All scars, it was, like twisted braids, and with a hole on the left, over the ribs. They cried, hugged, kissed each other, and for the first – and the last – time, they sat down and split a bottle between them.

Those two combat veterans were never friends, and they never matched up decorations and medals again, but on Victory Day, as is right and proper, they went to the quiet little village cemetery, where, each on his own, they grinned to themselves as a speaker sent from the regional center stood below a soldier statue painted silver, and crumpled the pages of his speech while he droned on and on, like he'd learned this by rote long ago, about the victory and the enormous losses. The villagers clapped, glancing over at the old campaigners, but everything those two had lived through seemed far-away and boring, like the black-and-white movies put on at the club. Yet the two old-timers were seeing, as if not a day had gone by, the mutilated people, the eyes mad with grief, the charred earth. And they said nothing.

PETROV GOES BACK TO SCHOOL

The Sheshurino school was shut down on the very cusp of the New Year. The last remotely literate teacher had bolted, taking with him Lenka Pereverzeva, a secondary school graduate, and the funds collected for roof repairs, and a stack of study guides. Stunned by such unexpectedly shabby treatment, the school started declining before our eyes, growing faded and ugly like an abandoned wife.

A commission that could not have cared less drove in from the district center and had whatever was still fit for classroom use loaded into the light truck known affectionately as a *polutorka*, also hauling off two barns'-full of split firewood, a likeness of Alexander Pushkin painted in oils during the reign of Tsar Nicholas, and the bell that had summoned the students to class. The commissioners walked around the frog-green building that sprawled across the state farm's land, rapped on its foundation and prodded at its planks, while the less trusting among them even tried to smash the flimsy wooden door frames.

"No, Pavel Ivanych," said the boss-lady, head of the District Education Department. "You can strike me dead on the spot, but we won't be able to write this piece of junk off, or sell it either. We'll have to scrap it and split the land into lots."

Pavel Ivanych always had a canny eye for the bottom line. "Isn't it a pity, though?" he said. "This place is built like a fortress. Stonework all across the first floor. And where are the kids going to go?"

"Where? To Kashurino. It has an eight-grade school. There aren't that many kids, anyway."

Pavel Ivanych took a swig from the flask he'd been keeping warm in his boot, shrugged his shoulders, and, as part of his goodbyes to the principal, Alexandra Nikitishna, who was all bundled up in a short shawl and crying her eyes out, told her to post a guard. "Or just someone to run the furnace," he added. And he made himself scarce.

There was nothing to run the furnace with, though, because they'd carted all the firewood away, so when Alexandra Nikitishna begged old man Petrov to keep an eye on the school at least until spring, that's exactly what he wanted to know – what to use for fuel. He'd already done the rounds of both floors and peered into the cellar.

"Is there some furniture dumped anywhere?" he asked. "They've swiped all the firewood."

"Use books for fuel," the principal said, blowing her nose into a white handkerchief. "The whole cellar's full of nothing but books."

But old man Petrov, a conscientious and thoughtful fellow, wouldn't hold with that kind of wanton destruction on his watch. After instructing his mother-in-law to keep the farm (which consisted entirely of a cow called Little Girl) up and running, he went to scout the felling sites and in a week had filled one of the barns to the rafters with burnable wood. Then he patted himself on the back for keeping socialist property out of capitalist hands, got the sturdy cylindrical stove good and hot, making the fresh aluminum paint bubble like a puddle in a July rainstorm, and started an asset inventory. The discarded books in the cellar

seemed alive to him. Installing himself on a bundle tied with twine, he pulled the top one of a pile toward him.

"This is your ninth-grade physics!" Petrov licked his finger. "Hoo boy, the know-how they've crammed in here! See how wisely the Lord set everything up, but this textbook was written by Rozenberg and Pushkarev... Figure that one out! Still, I'd have too hard a time with physics just now. When was I called up into the army? There you go, then! So I'll start by getting a handle on my native language."

Petrov liked the language book. It had pictures of fields of rye, birds flying in the sky, and a photo of Laktionov's painting *A Letter from the Front*. His eyes filled with tears, and he lit a cigarette. When his ma had gotten his pa's death notification, she'd beaten Verka, the mail lady, with her own mailbag and then they'd sat and bawled, two women with one voice. And it was cold, and the hunger was something fierce.

He turned a page. Haymaking – now that's the ticket! Such a good time it was. Back then, Grandma Pelageya would fill an earthenware jug with milk from the day-time milking, wrap it in a cloth, and hand out baked spuds and home-made bread. Petrov would whistle to the dog, and off they'd go, through the woods. The dust was warm and the puddles had started drying up, but they'd still be home to some tiny frogs. So he'd weave burdock thistle stems together, heads and all, skewer the froglets on them, and pop them into his basket. And later, out on the hayfield, he'd wait until Valka, the screechiest woman in the village, was nodding off against a haystack, and then he'd drop them down her smock. Such a good time. Pictures of an earlier life, happy as only youth can be, floated before Petrov's eyes, combining into multicolored clouds like balloons...

It took him a week to separate the books by the effect they had on him. He ended up with six stacks. There was one that nobody should live without, that had every-thing – sowing turnips, assembling a rifle, splicing wires without getting killed, and astronomy. The second pile was all dictionaries, a murky business, and how to adapt it to real life, Petrov did not know. The books in the third were well-worn and tat-tered, with a portrait of Lomonosov or Tolstoy scrawled over in ink – they would make good cigarette papers. The fourth and fifth – *Vitya Maleyev in School and at Home, Styopa the Hare, Anna Karenina* – were to be read. Petrov had them all at the ready, for broadening his mind after sundown in winter. And the sixth was a gold-mine of maps, and, oh, so very useful! Petrov even found Budapest, which he'd last visited in a tank. But there was no mention of Sheshurino anywhere, so small it was in the great global expanse.

And the evenings passed – long in winter, just a tad shorter in spring – as old man Petrov made his way through all the school's learned lore by the light of a kerosene lamp and the cheery crackle of the stove as it crunched up the brushwood.

THE PATTY SHOP

Jolting along mud-choked roads, sending up spurts of brownish ooze, the district bus is clambering up and down the humpbacked hillocks. Bursting at the seams, it wallows on, rolling from side to side, past tiny villages strung like beads along the roadway. At every bead, which is marked by a rusty shack made lopsided by time, a woman hikes up her skirts to scramble out, invariably stepping straight into a deep puddle and swearing up a storm at Kolka, the driver. The passengers still on the bus spread out more comfortably, wipe the fogged-up windows with the elbows of their quilted jackets, and take out calico carriers that now, in place of the jars of milk that had been sold at the market, hold chunks of liver sausage that smell dispiritingly, and to high heaven, of garlic.

Spreading cloths across their plump knees, they break off the crusty ends of not-quite-black bread, peel boiled eggs, and produce from inside their coats the dark wine bottles they call fire extinguishers. They drink straight from the bottle, wiping the pinkish trickle from their chins with their sleeves. The old fellows sitting in the back are blowing cigarette smoke into their sleeves, clumsily waving the gray clouds away. They're dressed for winter already, in thick, home-knitted turtleneck sweaters, greasy quilted jackets, and gray three-flap hats from their army days.

The bus pitches to one side for the umpteenth time. A piglet tied up tightly in a sack gives a grunt, and chickens jammed into a basket with a checkered cloth tied around the top cackle.

The bus bogs down. Grudgingly tossing their cigarettes away, the old lads poke at the youngsters who've been rocked to sleep by the jolting, and the womenfolk, young and old, get out to lighten the bus's load. Branches are cut from roadside trees and chocked under the wheels to turn the waterlogged road into an impromptu timber track. Everyone's chilly out here, so a bottle makes the rounds again. Now the youngsters are wide awake and off they go, laughing, talking over past adventures, spinning tall tales, and singing songs, because this trip hasn't been much fun so far.

"Yagorna!"

"Huh?"

"Yagorna, how come you're not stone dead yet? How old are you, anyway?"

"Let up, won't you? You're still wet behind the ears, Natakha, but I used to be in the Komsomol. In a Komsomol cell... Time was, someone'd play a 'cordion, and we'd sing and sing..."

"Aren't you all sung out yet? I bet you don't even roll off your nice warm stove bench before noon..."

One of the oldsters puffs on his hand-rolled cigarette. "It's about time she bit the dust," he says. "What do I keep telling her? She needs to make a hole in the ceiling, to make it easier, you know, for her soul to escape – unless her backside gets stuck."

The womenfolk pass the wine around, chattering on about the children and how there's no breathing in the bus, what with the sheep's wool making your eyes smart and all.

"Pull up, Kolka!" the oldest of them yells. "So the old lads can take a dump, and we can stretch our legs."

Kolka obediently pulls off to the side of the road, and the bus empties, leaving only the piglet grunting under a seat...

The very last stop on the route was the patty shop in the village of Serezhkino. It was as dark as could be when the bus got in, the deep gloom of five o'clock on a fall evening. The villagers had packed the dining room by that hour, the menfolk coming from work and the womenfolk from the farm. They'd arrived in families, solemnly, bringing their children, to buy them lemonade and cookies. The customers swarmed around the counter like flies, and the server – Klava, a mature lady with a bust large enough to balance full wine-glasses on as steady as you please – swiveled her queenly head adorned with fake ruby earrings this way and that, yelling "Back away!," "Paws off!," and "What d'you think the price tags are for?"

Klava handed the goods out following a criterion known only to her. She let this one run up a tab, and had that one thrown out on his ear, and treated this other one to a friendly grin, baring the angular gold caps on her teeth.

The beer was supplied in milk cans and was brewed close by, at the bakery. The menfolk waited for it, milling around in a separate little flock and listen-

ing for a telltale noise outside the window. With a twitch of her eyebrows Klava would send two especially trustworthy guys out when the truck arrived, to roll the heavy aluminum containers down a plank. And that's when a scene of confusion right up there with the collapse of the Tower of Babel began to unfold. The men crowded in, crawling over each other and dropping their money, while Klava, her slitted eyes sunk into her bulldog cheeks, ladled the beer out into mugs. There was a fresh smell, like in a banya.

"Don't expect any topping off!" Klava snapped. "We're draining these cans mighty fast. And no, I'm not pouring any into your jars."

Her hands, their thick fingers painted with crimson nail polish, smartly counted out the damp change from a plate holding coins. At last the beer crowd took its seats, pushing the tables together and laying out the skimpy district newspaper with its murky photos of renowned combine operators, and started banging silvery pieces of dried fish against the table tops, so the scales would come off easier. The first mug was drunk in a reverent silence, with much sucking on the fish, closely followed by a second mug, and a third. Then somebody pulled out from under the table a bottle of vodka and slopped it lavishly into the mugs, to beef up the beer. They lit up too. None of the cigarette butts were stamped out on the plank floor, though. Instead they were collected in the empty bottle, which proceeded to smoke like a volcano.

The family men were seated away from all that. They dug their forks into their beetroot salads while the womenfolk dropped their thick wool headscarves onto their shoulders, wiped the sweat from their brows, blew on their glasses of tea, and tore into buns stuffed with fruit puree or rice. They didn't throw the crusts away but popped them into wide-open pockets, for the birds at home. The older gals were partial to the dried-fruit drinks, which they picked up from a tray, carried over to a table, tottering all the way, and drank matter-of-factly, cramming the sticky apple and apricot slices into their toothless mouths. The little kids scampered among the tables, begging for candy or kopeks, and then dragged a kitten in from the street and played hide and go seek under the tables.

The patty shop's greatest claim to fame was, of course, its hot meat patties. The young divorcée Lyubka, Klava's assistant, made them in house, and put so much of her love and hopes for marriage into them that they came out extra special, so tasty that people took them home for special occasions and for no particular reason at all.

Flies buzzed merrily beneath the ceiling and settled unenthusiastically on the sticky fly strips, but no one paid them any attention. A little mouse had a nibble on a sack of flour and scuttled away – but this was the countryside, so the cat was right on it.

They sat there long and impassively until the last bus was ready to leave, as signaled by the bus driver barking into the dining room, "Finish up, guys, we gotta go." Flashing a happy smile, Klava poured him a nice brimming mugful with a chaser and gave him a patty hot from the oven, because in her line of work, her earnings depended on whoever was driving the bus... The other drivers who were spending the night somewhere near the patty shop were still sitting around, but our folks, pushing each other's quilted behinds, got back on, and the bus, cheerfully breathing out stale booze and garlic from the patties, and unsteady as a pregnant sheep, sloshed its way along the mud-choked roads of Russia as the gray murk gathered outside the windows.

GRANDPA CUCKOO

Vaska Solovyov, nicknamed "Cuckoo" because he stuttered whenever he said "coo-coo-could…," was puzzled. And the puzzle was how to come up with the money he needed to throw a shindig. Which, for those who don't know, has nothing to do with the bone below the knee or what you need a shovel for: it's a big spread put on to celebrate something, and it has to involve wine and vodka.

This shindig would be to see Sashka, Vaska's grandson, off to St. Petersburg. Sashka had worked the last nerve of everybody in the village. Who knows how much gas he'd siphoned from people's cars and trucks, how many bicycles, spare parts, and other good stuff (hidden well away by some summer visitor from the city) he'd filched? Sure, he'd been given a good beat down right there on the spot any number of times, but that just toughened him up. Tough enough for the army, he was. But they didn't take the likes of him – no fools, they.

"He's a %&*#, and that's all he is," the chief army recruiter said. "He'd demolish all of the armed forces, and they've yet to come up with a war we could hustle that little brat off to without being scared on the enemy's behalf. No need to drop a bomb – he'd wreak havoc on their military single-handed. And he couldn't be issued a weapon, either, never mind a tank. He'd sneak off to a dance in it, or worse."

So Vaska had a word with Lenka, Sashka's mother, and decided that the boy needed to go to the city they all called "Piter." Country folk had been setting themselves up in Piter for ever and a day, and with good jobs too – some running excavators, some operating bulldozers – and every one of them was making great money. Besides, they were straight arrows, family men, so they wouldn't put up with anybody's nonsense, and there was nothing to steal. The kid wouldn't bother them, not one bit. At least, that's how Cuckoo figured it.

"I'd like to send him to the moon, that moocher," Lenka said after giving it some thought. "Except he'd mess their rocket up and sell it off. Right there in space."

СААЧИ
НЕТ

"They could make a satellite out of him, couldn't they?" Cuckoo wondered to himself. "The state would get some use out of that, and it'd be nice to be down here in the village and see him flying across the starry sky, all twinkling colors."

They made the rounds of the kinfolk and scared up the money for a one-way train ticket to Piter. The kinfolk were eager to give and didn't even want anything back. They couldn't believe their luck. Barns burned, Hawberry the horse stolen, live chickens plucked bare, and rabbits sold straight out of their cages – all this made the kinfolk generous.

"Pops, you need to loosen the purse strings too," Lenka hinted. She'd been out of a job for the past seven years.

"Your purse strings are already loose enough for the both of us," Cuckoo replied. He did get a pension, but in the new-fangled way, on a gaudy plastic rectangle. Nasty it was, so humiliating. Cuckoo had even forbidden himself to think about it. He'd go to get some wine, and grouchy old Afonikha, a heifer if ever he'd seen one, would mark it down in her notebook as an IOU. Vaska suspected that she was padding his account too, because the money he paid her should have been enough to keep him so hammered he'd be seeing pink elephants by now. But if he handed his plastic pension card to Lenka, he'd lose the lot of it, that he knew for sure, and he didn't care to go bouncing around in the cold innards of a bus on a fifty-miles trip to spend his pension in town.

Vaska decided to set some pike traps. He put on his snug felt boots with overshoes from a chemical hazmat suit and high-tailed it to the lake. And then, after bartering the pike he'd caught for bread, wine, a big hunk of lard, and a fresh but wrinkly cucumber, Cuckoo sent out the invitations.

Everybody in the village came. They set up tables in the big room, but then they had to put some in the kitchen and the overflow even snaked into the corridor. And still some people were standing as they drank. (Somebody had brought some very decent moonshine.) The womenfolk sang about Chapayev, the menfolk talked about the fish not biting right then and how there'd be no war. Lenka was sobbing into a curtain, but she didn't really mean it. They reminisced about Sashka's shenanigans. After a swig of wine from a tea cup with mauve flowers on it, Lenka suddenly remembered Sashka helping one of the old gals chop firewood and how well he did it, even though the ax was as big as him.

Then everyone started getting dewy-eyed. Granny Dunya remembered how Sashka stole a full bag of mandarin oranges that she'd bought for the children's Christmas party at school, and he wouldn't own up to it. And then he'd broken out in spots, and everybody was onto him right away, but he was scratching and crying so hard, they didn't beat him bad, just locked him up for a bit. Auntie Valya, the neighbor, ransacked her memory too and, blowing her nose on her caftan sleeve, told how Sashka had helped her stack firewood. "And what was the big deal about that?" asked Auntie Valya, flashing a toothless smile. "Because he only took a hundred rubles for it."

Cuckoo stood up from the table but only part way. "Why, that son of a gun!" he said. "The school wanted them doing good turns for free, like the Pioneers used to. He even got a certificate for it."

"Oh, give it a rest!" Auntie Valya brandished her glass and fished a sprat from its can. "Now Piter can go ahead and pay him for stacking their wood."

From firewood they went on to prices, then they had a little scuffle, and by midnight the party had broken up. They all shook Cuckoo's hand as they left, so long and hard his shoulder started aching. The womenfolk kissed Lenka, smearing their lipstick all over her cheeks.

Grandpa Cuckoo got up the next morning still a tad tipsy but light of soul, because they'd finally got rid of the grandkid. The cuckoo had foisted its fledgling off onto another bird. Let them raise him; Grandpa had had enough. Now it was Piter's turn to shiver and shake. "He'll show them cop series of theirs a thing or two," Grandpa thought gleefully to himself. But he was so busy celebrating, he'd missed just one thing – that nobody had actually spotted young Sashka at the going-away party...

In the dense darkness before dawn, young Sashka had been using his grandpa's hacksaw to cut through a puny Chinese padlock that a skittish summer visitor had hung on his boat shed. The hacksaw was doing good work, but the buyers from a republic down south were already waiting out there on the road, smoking, their elbows resting on an eggplant-colored Zhiguli station wagon with a trailer...

Sashka was bending the shackle back. "I'll give them Piter," he thought. "Or forget Piter, I'll just give them the finger." The money he was going to pocket plus the price of the tickets that the kinfolk had shelled out for would be plenty to finance another month of fun and games, and Ma and Grandpa Cuckoo could like it or lump it.

RASPBERRY BEETLES

Moonshine has always been made in the countryside – under our Tsar-Father, and when the revolution was on, and during the official crackdown on alcohol. Sure it has, because it's stronger than the ruble and safer than gold. And, truth be told, it's simple enough to make, though there is a trick to it. What's the main thing? To get a good mash going. That's the basis of the process, and there's nothing here that's not important. Put simply, you mix yeast and sugar then pour in some warm water, following the proportions in the recipe. After that it's like caring for a little tot, which means keeping it warm, even wrapping it in a blanket. You can also sprinkle in peas or some sort of grain, so it'll have more bubbles. And after a week or so, you're in business – fire up the stove, and then everyone does it his own way. Two cast-iron containers are set up, one on top of the other, with a coiled tube stuck between them. The containers are smeared with raw dough, to send the mash, when it boils, into the tube. The tube goes down into a washtub and this is where ... Oh no you don't! You stay right there! You have to keep topping it up with cold water, because that's what makes the moonshine such a wonder. People who are especially picky about quality will add milk to it next. That "settles" it, making it come out clean and without that raw booze smell. Milk's like charcoal: it attracts the fermentation by-products, so they stay in the bottom of the jar.

My neighbor Nadyukha – a well-heeled old thing of fifty or so who worked as a cook at the local hospital – was apt to turn to drink whenever fate got her down. Which would be on her days off. After a visit to the banya. On Fridays, I would give her the whey from my curd cheese to feed her cows, taking some milk in return. One time, though, I'd been brewing moonshine for my guests. I poured the milk in it and left it in the closet to clarify. But then I went and mixed up the jars. And gave Nadyukha a good six pints of pure alcohol.

I was woken in the morning by a knock at the window. Nadyukha was standing by the porch post, in a colorful housecoat that was inside-out. The post was damp with the morning dew and Nadyukha's tears. Her face was frazzled, and her feet were bare.

"Let me have a hair of the dog, Darya ... I'm dying right in front of you ... You'll never be able to forgive yourself if you don't."

"You've no shame, coming to me for a hair of the dog! How did you get that tanked, anyway?"

Nadyukha was sober for just an instant; the next second, she grabbed the post like it was a stripper pole and crashed to the ground.

"Oh my stars!" Nadyukha hollered. "But I... I... I was thinking it's whey. I poured it into the cow's drinking trough!"

"And how's the cow doing?" I asked tartly.

"She wouldn't go out to the herd... And the sheep are all drunk. I wondered what they were sick with!"

"Your sniffer's good – how come you didn't smell it? It's pure alcohol!"

"Have you ever been in a cowshed?" Nadyukha asked, keeping a firm grip on the post. "What does it smell like? There you go, then."

And she fell flat on her face and dozed off in the rays of the rising sun.

After that I started marking the jars with circles and crosses. To avoid what you might call an unrecoverable beverage error.

I have a big family, so there's plenty of drinking done here without Nadyukha's help. And my sibling's kids were going stir crazy in Moscow, so to take the pressure off a bit, their parents started sending them to spend the summer with me. They rampaged through the thickets and tried to take the cow out to pasture, and their parents would come on their days off. For a drink and a snack. They used to drink straight vodka, but that costs money. So then they started pounding down the moonshine, leaving their kids bored stiff and fed up.

The sad little tykes had found a copy of the old *Healthy Lifestyle* newsletter in the attic. I didn't know that when they came to me and asked, "Auntie Dasha, where can we get some raspberry beetles?"

"Catch some ordinary beetles and paint them," I said. I thought they were going to play toy soldiers.

"Nu-uh! They'll flake it off..."

And that got me seriously worried.

"Auntie Dasha," the youngest, six-year-old Sonya, said in her feather-light voice, "what's a *shtof*?"

"About a third of a gallon," I said without thinking, then went cold with horror. It couldn't be: the kids had started drinking vodka too?

"Now I'm going to want some answers, my little chicks – who have you decided to poison, your pops or yourselves?"

The children went all sheepish and brought me the newsletter. The recipe for "Madame Filstein's Nostrum against Drunkenness, 1909" was simple: "Take one glass of raspberry beetles and a *shtof* of vodka. Steep them together in a cool, dark place, give two small wine glasses at lunch, and your husband will be sober FOR-EVER." It sounded menacing. But the big surprise was that the children hadn't also asked me to supply them with a bottle of the good stuff..

After catching a glassful of beetles in the bushes, the children put the vodka in a dark place ... and then the summer was over. The next spring I found the bottle, now containing a vile-smelling slush. Yes indeed, a swig of that would definitely make any-one's husband turn up his toes on the spot – no prizes for guessing that.

And just then, our own prize specimen showed up. Nadyukha.

"Hair of the dog... I'm dying..."

"Nadya," I told her straight, "I've got some. But you'll never drink again."

"Hand it over!"

"Then it's on you."

After scraping the beetles out of the glass with her little finger, Nadyukha knocked it back with a flourish, grimaced, lit up a cigarette, and said, "@%#$, that's some fine cognac! Hand it over, all of it."

After a week of watching Nadyukha coming and going, I figured out that the beetles only work on men. Something to do with testosterone, probably...

TAKING NAMES AND TELLING TALES

The little village of Klyuchi settled on the shores of the Pustoshka River in the late nineteenth century. The soil wasn't the richest in those parts, but the vegetable plots never failed, bringing forth potatoes, turnips, carrots, and flax like clockwork, and the cows had plenty of pasture in the flood-meadows alongside the river. The womenfolk bore children, spun, milked the cows, churned butter, and wove unusually lovely striped floor mats that were made nowhere else. The menfolk went to the nearest town for seasonal work – hard workers they were and skilled in the carpenter's craft. So the village lived on and knew no hardship.

The revolution and the war wiped out almost all the men, and the collective farm destroyed the private farming. In the late twentieth century, the collective farm fell apart too, laying bare more misfortune and wrongdoing than the revolution itself had, because people were now left without even the paltry, albeit regular, wages they'd had before. Only thirty-six homes still stood in Klyuchi, compared to four hundred at the start of the century before.

The huts were no less well made than they'd ever been, crafted from local larchwood, but time had shown no mercy to them either. They went visibly lopsided, and the roofs decayed, and the glass cracked in the windows, which had gone all askew too, so they looked more like diamonds than rectangles.

In the very center of the village was the home of Natalya Mitrofanova – a sturdy hut with lacy wooden casings around its windows and a brick chimney that puffed out white smoke in winter. Stesha, Natalya's sleek cow, would be mooing in the barn while two dozen chickens roamed the yard and a piglet, pink with black spots, oinked away in her little sty. Natalya was retired but still a strong old thing who managed all on her own, hiring folk only to split the firewood or mow the hay.

КИЛЬКА
VLADIMIR SHAKESPEARDŪ

But Tolya Kryuchkov lived on the far fringes of Klyuchi, close to what had been the collective farm's granary. He was of an age with Natalya, but his hut had settled into the ground, the roof was mottled, with patches of tar paper showing, and the only other living thing it sheltered was a villainous-looking black cat.

Tolya was maimed, missing fingers on his left hand, but he'd fixed it so he could do simple jobs, helping himself out with a shoulder here, an elbow there. His pension was beggarly, yet he wouldn't ever work for Natalya, because their families had been at odds from way back. The Mitrofanovs had been riffraff and hard drinkers, but came up in the world during the revolution, when they ran amok through the master's house and lands, looted churches, hollered at rallies, and herded their fellow villagers into the collective farm, sensing that for them there was a living to be made there while doing nothing but yelling themselves hoarse and being generally despicable.

The Kryuchkovs, though, were Old Believers, people of the land. They worked nonstop and prayed, kept strictly to the old ways, and never bowed to the new authorities. They flat out refused to join the collective farm and steered clear of the rallies. And for that, they paid the price.

Vaska Mitrofanov, Natalya's grandfather, didn't even bother to put anything in writing. He just made a verbal report that this spawn of the illicitly wealthy peasantry, these priest-loving Old Believers, these stubborn individualists were bad-mouthing Soviet power, and whatever they were plotting, it wasn't good. That was all it took. Tolya's grandfather was shot on the spot, without trial, but his father was tried and transported to the Ustvymlag prison camp, where he felled timber right up until the war began. He left for the front just as soon as his release papers arrived, but he never came back. Informed on by a member of military intelligence, he was shot as a traitor, because he was forever praying to God and wouldn't shave his beard.

The Kryuchkovs' home was commandeered for "the needs of the collective farm" (it became the head office), and to this very day, whenever Tolya walks by it, he looks away and clenches his right hand, his five-fingered hand, so tightly that the fist turns red. Tolya's mother, along with Tolya and his sisters, were taken in by distant kinfolk who themselves were hard up, but still had a crust of bread to share with them and a roof to put over their heads.

When Tolya's mother died, he decided to return to his native village, so as not to be a burden on his kin. Klyuchi had had a hard time getting on its feet after the war, so broken-backed and hungry it was. It howled aloud, a chorus of woe, yet it slowly but steadily came back to life. And Tolya made his home in an abandoned hut and scraped along as best he could. He was taken on as a tractor driver in no time, though, for all that he was just a little squirt who could hardly clamber up onto the running board.

Natalya's Grandpa Vasily, being a Party man, had a military exemption, meaning that the front had had to make do without him. And her father quickly figured out where he could get by while also indulging the spite he'd been born with. So he signed up with the NKVD, where he got lots of blood on his hands – and not enemy blood, either.

Natalya, her mother, grandmother, and younger brothers were going through hard times too. But she'd been endowed with her grandfather's knack of knowing who to cozy up to if she wanted to live the high life, and that entailed joining the Komsomol and, in due time, the Party. Where she was everyone's worst nightmare. She'd call people on the carpet for tiny offenses, she'd tell them off, she'd talk menacingly about knowing where the bodies were buried. Worse, she wasn't squeamish about tattling in the appropriate quarters about who'd taken the farm's milk home for a sick child, who'd picked up frozen potatoes from the farm fields, who hadn't shown up for the mowing, claiming to be ill, who was brewing moonshine... The long and short of it was that they'd all done something they needed to confess to the authorities, and that could well earn them a trip – a trip far, far away.

Natalya probably didn't even know that her grandfather had hounded the Kryuchkov family to hell and back, but she was wary of Tolya, sensing that he harbored some secret grudge, a hidden malice toward her. Still, worse luck for her, she liked him, a whole lot. And why not, seeing as how nicely he'd filled out. No longer the same skinny little boy, all sharp angles, he was broad in the shoulder now, with strong hands and a ramrod-straight back. His eyes were gray, his lashes thick, his gaze bold and defiant. She'd try to cozy up with him now and then. Let's go dancing, she'd say, or to a movie at the club, but he'd just shrug and never speak a word. Natalya wasn't the timid sort, though. She knew how to have her way, and she wasn't one to stand on ceremony with the boys. So she went for it, getting ahold of Tolya one time in the hay barn, breathing moonshine fumes into his face, and telling him, straight out, if you don't want to be mine, you'll be sorry... But he pushed her away and tacked on a rude name for good measure.

Natalya bit her lip, and in no time at all, a letter – anonymous of course, but written in a round hand the authorities recognized – took flight. "I hereby bring to your attention," it said, "that Kryuchkov, Anatoly, is a parasite on society, steals wood from the logging site, works illegally on the side, and has fallen into moral decay."

The first thing they did was drag Tolya before the district committee, where it turned out that he wasn't one of them at all. He hadn't even been in the Komsomol. They laid into him, but he stood firm, so Natalya poured more oil on the fire, and they sentenced him, without rhyme or reason, to five years. Give them the man and they'll make the case, as people used to say.

Tolya served out his time, then he wandered the country, saved his money, and came back home to Klyuchi, though the Klyuchi he'd known was all but gone. He came back missing fingers. The penal colony was no health resort, for sure, but on top of that he was sick, a sick man through and through. And his house was all slanted.

Natalya, meanwhile, was in clover, living on her pension, and it was a good one, too. She hadn't quit writing denunciations, sending up red flags, you might say, to the newspaper or to the prosecutor's office, but in times like these, who was going to listen to an old pensioner lady? Still, she was scared of writing anything about Tolya Kryuchkov.

And that's how they live to this day, pretty much eyeball to eyeball. Natalya's afraid of Tolya, because heaven help her if he were to come and burn her house down for spite, like they used to in the old days. But Tolya never says a word, though he wonders to himself how the earth can bear the weight of people like her. He has granted forgiveness for his mutilated life, but for what happened to his grandfather, and his father and mother – that he will never forgive.

THE COMMUNITY COURT

The notice pinned to the general store door was written in ballpoint pen. "Club, October 12, 5 p.m. Community Court. Agenda Item 1: The Conduct of Nikolayev, N. N." it said, and it was signed "The Rural Council." And then, written sideways in the same hand: "Everybody who ordered gas, bring money."

The club was packed, leaving no room to breathe. Some people were smoking in the vestibule; the kiddies were scampering between the rows of seats; the womenfolk, dressed warmly, smelled of soap and damp sheepskin. The rural council chairman, who was also the head engineer at the timber company, came flying in, throwing off his jacket on the way and losing papers out of his file. He banged his fist on the table, yelled at Tosya, the accountant, to take the minutes, and started things off.

"So, comrades, we have come here today to judge Nikolayev, Nikolai, for striking his mother-in-law, Grandma Valya (Petrova, Valentina, that is), in the face. Go ahead, Nikolayev, speak your piece!"

Up onto the stage came the scrawny Nikolayev, an eternally crestfallen, vinegary little man, a tightwad and a drunk.

"Whaddya mean? I never hit her. What kind of a jerk am I? It was her... I'd been out in the forest, bone-tired I was, and she'd poured out my vodka, a whole pint of it... What the..? I says. Me and Gramps, we'd wanted a bit of guy-time... And then, to top it off, Gramps was mightily ticked off at me, that he was..."

"Well, if she poured it out, that wasn't good," the chairman agreed. "It's because she's not evolved. That's not how it's done, for sure. But smacking her in the face there, Kolya?"

"Yeah, well...," Nikolayev was squirming. "What did I want? I wanted to pop her on the butt with the rolling pin, that's what."

A noisy stir ran through the audience. Nikolayev's mother-in-law had a butt that would give the rear end on Boy the horse a run for its money.

Loud shouts from the front rows: "A rolling pin's only good for flattening dough on that butt of hers!"

"She dodges me," Kolya droned on. "And clacks her teeth at me like nobody's business, so I drops the rolling pin. She goes to get it, my hand comes up and cracks her in the eye."

"That's bad, Kolya," the chairman scolded him in fatherly tones. "I mean, she's still a broad, for all that she's your ma-in-law. Admit that you were wrong, and we'll let it go. But we'll dock her what she's owed for picking cranberries. You got that down, Tosya? That's it, then – let's collect the gas money. Off home now, people. Tomorrow we've got two work teams going to Okhonya. Somebody's downed some timber there and left it lying." And with that, the chairman wound up the meeting.

Nikolayev went out for a smoke, crushed out his cig in a huff, and took off with the lads from the timber company's vehicle pool to the canteen, where he could spin the "incident" to make himself look good.

Back at home, his mother-in-law, sensing disaster in the air, hurriedly collected the oven forks and the pots, hid the poker, and shamefacedly set the table. With a pint of vodka. After that, she scoured the yard with her eyes and, seeing no sign of Nikolayev, went back inside and carried on doing what she usually did.

S-s-swoosh! The snow slid off the right side of the roof, which had been warmed by the stove. Nikolayev's mother-in-law tore her eyes from the television. It was a stylish TV, flat and inconvenient. The other one, a box model, had quite conveniently held a plaster Lenin and a cat-shaped coin bank decorated with flowers. This one Seryozha (her big-city son-in-law) had screwed right into the wallpaper, so Lenin had to be put in the sideboard for safekeeping. The old gal listened hard, to hear if her son-in-law was coming, yawned, peeked at the icon corner, where the holy countenance of *The Joy of All Who Sorrow, With Alms Coins* glowed bright, and made the sign of the cross over her mouth. She was wearing a pair of the fleecy leggings that soft-hearted Chinese people had been sending in random sizes to the Russian countryside. "Shame on them," the mother-in-law thought. "What sort of size is that? Three rude-looking letters – XXL... What are they getting at?"

She wrapped herself in her fluffy flannel robe and went back to rolling a six-pint jar of cream with her bare foot. Valya had calculated that after seven episodes of her show, she would have a jar full of churned butter, which would justify the electricity she'd used up in the meantime.

On the table, waiting for her son-in-law, the pint bottle stood in a sweat, the salted cucumbers were wilting and the pickled cabbage was getting overly tangy. Grandpa Arkhipych, Nikolayev's father-in-law, was on the outs with his wife and had taken to bed in the main room, still wearing his greasy padded pants and body warmer as a mark of protest. Grandma Valya kept glancing vengefully at the snowy-white dust ruffles all smudged with grime and said not a word.

"He needs more than a good locking-up," Gramps yelled peevishly. "It'd be a relief to everybody. Silly old fool that you are, you could have gotten rid of him for a spell. But you went and took him my money, so's they wouldn't lock him up, the scumbag. And he should've been tried and locked up. Let him pay you for putting your face out of whack."

"I gave it 'cos I had to," the old gal said, not taking her eyes from the TV. "If they lock him up, who's going to feed Lena and the little ones? You?"

"What's it to do with me? Maybe I was saving that money for a motorsickle, to cheer me up in my old age? A kopeck here makes a ruble there... Me, I didn't drink... I'm done now, so shut up. I'm dying here."

"Die, then, you old divvil. So much of my blood you've drunk, worse than that son-in-law."

The old gal got up and looked through the window again. Nikolayev was still carousing out there somewhere. She clinked around in the cupboard, splashed some of the hard stuff into a glass, gulped it down, grunted, gave Gramps a sideways look, and said, "Don't bother getting up, there's still plenty here to serve at your wake."

Arkhipych started blubbering at that, hopped up from the couch, pushed the old gal out of way, and drained the rest of the bottle in one go. Then he mellowed out, slapped Valya on the posterior, and went off to split wood.

"It's way past time," the old gal said, sitting down on the sofa, switching to her right foot, and going back to rolling the butter.

Instead of waiting for that lowdown Nikolayev, Grandma Valya yelled at her daughter Lena to go pick up the eggs and, while she was at it, feed the cow its swill. After a bit of grumbling for appearance's sake, Lena stopped in the entryway to throw on a threadbare sheepskin coat donated by some seasonal visitors and went outside. Toward nightfall a thaw had come on, a softening... The path to the barn was melting, so she had to put boots on too.

Opening the door, Lena breathed in the thick, warm aroma brewed from hay, manure, and milk, and pushed away the chickens grubbing in the trough, telling them to be off and lay eggs because all they ever did was crap and crap some more and that's all they knew how to do. The chickens darted aside with a disgruntled clucking and settled on their perch to sleep, rocking to and fro in the warmth rising from the cow's back. Zorka the cow languidly chewed last year's hay and looked dejectedly up at the dingy little window set just below the roof. Lena poured the swill into the trough, put out more hay, collected the rough, cool eggs from the nests, and left, latching the barn door behind her.

Nikolayev didn't make it home much before daybreak and was so scared of payback from his mother-in-law that he bedded down in the barn, right there on the hay.

A WINTER'S TALE

For us out here in the country, winter is always a joy. Because, well, there's snow, and snow's always better than rain. Because when the hut's all covered with snow, it'll be warmer, like under a blanket. Minus twenty outside, the sun's shining like mad, throwing blue shadows across the white drifts. Thin tails of smoke drift upward from the chimneys, like someone's sitting in the stove with a cigarette and blowing the smoke up into the sky, a sure sign of a cold snap. In winter, no surprise here, everybody stays home, except the small fry. They have a blast, careering down all the hills, whooping it up, and shrieking. They ride their little sleds and those who don't have sleds slide on their behinds. And then there are all the dogs – even they're having fun.

But you have to dress special in winter. See, if you're in a city, there's subways and there's cars, so you could go barefoot or run around in your undies, there's no way you're going to freeze. Not in the country, though. Stick your nose out there, and you're done, it's darn near frozen off. The gals bundle themselves up in shawls. The one underneath is an ordinary cotton print and the one on top is a thin knit. For workaday life, either brown or gray, but for days off or to go to the club, a bleached, crocheted affair. No villager in living memory has ever worn a fur coat. Sheepskin jackets, yes. But they're heavy on the shoulders, which is fine for somebody on guard duty, where you're standing in one spot, or for a policeman. But our folks keep it simple – a quilted jacket and away you go.

Valenki are something else altogether. In Russia, those felt boots are as near as you can get to the number-one footwear, after regular leather boots. The old 'uns who used to roll the felt for *valenki* were held in high honor.

You need a sheep's fleece, but only from the spring shearing, and you have to prepare it just right. First you have to lay the whole thing out and give it a good eyeballing, let your experienced fingers feel what kind of fleece it is. Thick, or

poor and paltry? Then it goes on the wool carder. To this day there are still some barnlike outbuildings with comb-looking things called carders set up inside. You put the fleece on one, and that doohickey rakes it through, taking out all sorts of debris, and you end up with a sheet of wool. That's peeled off the carder, formed into a loose tube, and taken to the workshop. There they spread it flat on a table, divide it into equal pieces (one for the left foot, one for the right), and they stretch the wool out just so and then start beating it with a stick to make the wool cling together. That's called "fulling," which is *valyat* in Russian, and that's likely where the word *valenki* comes from.

Those artisans were also called *pimokaty* – *pima* rollers – sometimes, because *pimy* are *valenki,* but only up in the North. Our *valenki* makers were *valyalshchiki.* And so simple did their craft seem to these people that it gave rise to a saying "*Vanku valyat,*" which means to waste time trying to knock a Vanka (a roly-poly children's toy) over – to goof off, in other words. Also, *vanka* was the old Russian term for a reel – the kind used to wind the wool, I guess.

Anyway, the next thing they did was cook it in hot water, so the wool would shrink and pull together. And once the *valenki* forms dried, they had to be crushed and pummeled to make the felt sturdy, else it's a mess. The *valenki* would be good for nothing. Proper *valenki* should make a hollow sound, but the inside should be comfortable and soft to the feet.

There's no footwear more important than *valenki* in the countryside. You want to be the judge of that? Well, when it's cold, there isn't a boot, whether high or low-cut, that keeps the foot this warm. And there's something special in sheep's wool that actually heals the foot, and the felting holds the warmth in. If it's slushy, there's no doing without rubber overshoes, that's for sure. But once you've got your overshoes on, you're all set. You could bathe with your *valenki* on, if you wanted. And the main thing is that *valenki* never, ever wear out. If they get shabby or spring holes, you go to an old 'un, and he'll resole them for you, put a new bottom on, and you're good to go. Or you can cut the tops off, and now you've got a pair of house slippers, and may they be a joy to you.

But *valenki* are inconvenient in the city, except maybe for the kiddies. They're no good for mashing down on car pedals. It's taken for granted that you'll walk slow and steady when you've got a pair on, but in the city everyone's running. They're hot too, if you wear them for sitting-down work. In the country, you come home, brush them off, and put them on the stove to dry. There's even a little shelf on the stove just for that.

Only one of the old 'uns in our village had ever been a *valenki* roller, and that was Ivan Arkhipych. And he was respected as all get-out. Well on in years, but still nifty with his hands. And such a lively mind when it came to *valenki*, he'd even been known to put patterns on them if he was making them for a girl. For grown women, no. What would grown women want with that? They wear them with overshoes anyway. So he came out with different sorts of *valenki* – light ones, heavy ones... But the most complicated were for children's feet. That took craftsmanship and no mistake, so as not to rub the kid's foot raw but still leave some room to grow in the coming year.

Old Arkhipych himself had more grandkids than you could shake a stick at. The thing of it was, though, that when he was getting the hay in, there were no grandkids in sight, but when the cabbage and potatoes were dug and ready, they'd swoop in to snatch them up and head off with them back to the city. And they really liked *valenki*. They wanted them for themselves and their child's godmother and their daughter-in-law and their kids and grandkids. Arkhipych always obliged. How could he not help?

The old lad did have one little character flaw, and that was if you insulted him, didn't say thank you, acted disrespectful by not treating him to a glass of something, he'd roll you a thicker left boot and a thinner right one, so you'd waddle like a duck. But he could turn out the teeniest tiniest *valenki*, no bigger than the palm of your hand.

Antoshka was Grandpa's favorite. He was betwixt and between, only a couple of years old but a smart little tyke. One time, though, he pulled such a stunt as can't be told with a straight face. Grandma had given him her treasure box to play with, and one of the things in it was a string of beads. Antoshka up and broke the string, and the beads bounced right into the fleece that Granddad was rolling, and Arkhipych's eyes were so bad, he didn't notice. He handed the *valenki* to the customer, and the customer couldn't figure out why his *valenki* were all lumpy and bumpy. Another time Antoshka tossed Grandpa's pension into the big kettle. And there it boiled and got mixed in with the felted material. Such a scamp!

Grandpa carries him into the workshop and sits him down on a stool. Antoshka claps his hands; this he's enjoying. "Pop-pop, pop-pop," he yells. "Make me *katanki*!"

(*Katanki* are what we call *valenki*.) So Grandpa rolls him a pair of *valenki*. And he says, "He's gotta be launched like a ship at the next big snow." Because Arkhipych was in the navy during the war, but that's no place to be rolling *valenki*, right?

Yes, but it's not every day a grandkid hits that all-grown-up mark. So the family came and some neighbors too. Great-grandma was even taken down off the warm stove. She's blind as a bat and deaf as a post, but she was enjoying herself as well. Nadyukha, Antoshka's mama, dressed him up in fleece pants, and Grandma got all teary-eyed too, and came and gave him a pair of pure silk ankle socks to mark the big day.

Nadyukha tugged the *valenki* on, and everyone was just wowed by how nice they looked. They set Antoshka on the floor and waited for him to start marching. An agreeable smile on everybody's face; that house was one joyful place.

Antoshka stood, and stood, and fell over. He wasn't used to it, they decided. They put him on his feet again. He fell down again. Then they leaned him up against a wall, sort of at an angle. His mama had put him in a knit cap with a pompom like a rose, so pretty it was. But the little tot, even at an angle like that, tumbled over again.

"Take everything off," Grandpa grumbles. "He's got no business sweating like he's in a banya."

"We're not going to undress him, are we?" Grandma asks. The old gal wasn't keen on having to dress him all over again. Grandma walks around him, slaps herself on the forehead, and says, "It's clear as day what the trouble is. That panpon's tipping him over. It's heavy. Tear it off, and the deuce take it. He's not a little lass, he can do without a panpon. Here, pin this brooch on him."

Mishka Sparrowlegs tore the pompom off. But without the pompon, Antoshka promptly tumbled over faster than before. Arkhipych was taking it very hard, wondering to himself if his *valenki* were screwing things up. "My *valenki*," he says, "are top-notch. This little nipper's not of age to stand up yet. He'd best be crawling still." And he suggested bringing Antoshka's little sled into the hut, so he could be pulled over the floor mats. But Great-grandma, deaf as she was, would have none of that, because her own mama had woven those mats. And because it was a lost art.

And then the neighbor girl came running in from the street, frozen stiff. They'd forgotten her, and she'd been standing out there with the sled, waiting to take Antoshka for a ride. Her feelings were hurt, so they decided to give her tea, with honey. And then her mama came and her grandma, and before long all the neighbors had come traipsing in, what with this odd business going on and all. An hour later, the dust was flying; it was quite the blowout, believe you me. They started knocking 'em back, which is the thing to do any chance you get, because it's so warming. Then somebody brought an accordion, and the dancing started.

About then, Antoshka's mama remembered that her son was still standing up against the wall. Not a word, not even a sigh from him.

"Oh dear," she says, "I bet he needs to pee!"

But it was too late. He already had. Didn't need help with that. The old gals started undressing him, unwrapping him. They took off his jackets, his leggings, his socks, and, while they were at it, the *valenki* too. They were wet, which stands to reason, young as he was. So Grandma took them to dry on the stove, and out of the *valenki* fell ... a pacifier, sixteen rubles in change, five bottle corks, a matchbox, and a ping-pong ball.

"There you go," Grandpa said. "The *valenki* have nothing to do with it, and your panpon's got nothing to do with it either. The kid was up on tiptoe."

SOMEONE ELSE'S GRANNY

There's a bus that runs from our village to the nearest town. Not often, though – only when it feels like going and when there's gas, so that means the village folk are always helping each other out. If somebody's going to Toropets, they'll bring back a batch of bread or pick up medicines from the pharmacy or drop off a TV for repair.

Well, so our neighbor Vitalik – who's famous for having taken his car apart a couple of years ago but would never buy parts for it, on account of he's lazy and he's got no money – called my husband to tell him that this one granny was needing a ride to Toropets. The husband's face fell, but he agreed anyway. "She's not chatty, is she?" he asks.

"Not a bit of it," Vitalik replies. "She's such a quiet old thing. Tight-lipped, even, seeing as how she's stone deaf."

"Where's the pickup?" the husband asks.

"At the cemetery," Vitalik answers.

The husband goes all grim. "Isn't there special equipment for that?" he asks. "I mean to say, I'm scared of dead people, and besides, we're going for groceries. It's just awkward."

"Don't you fret," says Vitalik soothingly. "Granny's a sprightly one, being that she's alive and kicking, and so what if she's ninety-four? We've got a bench at the cemetery, right? And she'll be sitting on that bench from early in the morning, on the dot."

"Where do we drop her off?" the husband asked.

"In Toropets…" Vitalik began, then the call cut off. Our phones aren't like in the city. Here, the way it goes is the cell system only works when there's no clouds. Or snow. Or rain.

"We'll take her there, and as for where – it's not Moscow, is it? We'll figure it out." And the husband went to roust the dog out of the car. It sleeps there to keep from being disturbed.

In the morning the dust was still down, and the granny was right there, in plain sight. There she sat, wearing a headscarf and woolen stockings, striped ones, with warm booties on her feet and a cat in her lap. So the husband asks, "Are we taking the cat too?" Granny says nothing.

"It's probably a job lot – Granny plus cat," I say. "That's how grannies are, either knitting socks or stroking cats. And the cat doesn't weigh a ton, now, does it? The car can handle it."

The husband lifts the granny up and sits her in the back, so she won't be bumped too badly over the ruts. But the cat's not up for a road trip. What would she be doing in Toropets anyway? The mice are tiny there. And then the police might ask to see her passport, and where's a cat going to get one of those? There you have it! So off we go.

It's a really bumpy trip, and I keep looking back to see how Gran's doing. But she's curled up and fast asleep. The only thing is, she's snoring, and hard too. "What's it matter?" the husband says soothingly. "It's even good that she's snoring. It's her way of signaling that she's alive and breathing through her nose."

We arrive in Toropets, and the town's wheeling and dealing like mad, it being a market day. There's a jaw-dropping amount of trading going on. It's one big shopping mall, a superstore in the run-up to the holiday season. "Where to, Gramma?" the husband asks. She keeps mum. But she's wide awake now, because the jolting has stopped. So we give her a good looking-over: maybe there's a note pinned to her somewhere? Like on a parcel. From... To... Nope. The husband puts a call in to Vitalik, but he's out of range. Must be in the forest. Then where's the old lady going?

"Well," the husband says, "Toropets isn't Moscow. Let's just drive her around, and maybe there'll be the glimmering of an ancient memory. Or maybe somebody's looking for her with a sign, like at the airport."

"And exactly when did they close the airport?" I ask. "We've never even had one, have we? Let's drive her to the train station. Six of one, half a dozen of the other – that's a transport hub too." So we did.

All sorts of old gals are hanging out at the station too, sitting there in clusters. "Perhaps we should sit her with them, and someone'll recognize her," the husband says. He's upset because there's no one to look after our grandma, and it's getting toward lunchtime. He gets out of the car, opens the door, and mimes at her, something like, "Come on, Gran, toddle off to the train station and take a seat. Out with you, your pals are sitting over there, waiting for you." This is apparently where they keep all the grannies. But ours wants nothing to do with that. She glowers, puffs out her cheeks, gabbles something. Damned if we can understand it.

"This must be a prerevolutionary old gal," the husband says. "She's using a dialect from back then. They'd have done well to package her with a dictionary. Kinda like a phrase book."

But the grannies from the train station are selling all sorts of veggies, and they aren't happy about this granny of ours. They're not big on competition, so they're gabbling something too, and one even tosses a cucumber at us. "This is a clear and present danger," the husband says. "We could get beat up. Let's drive on." Which we do – for an hour, two hours... Granny's starting to have a fine old time, looking through the window and smiling. She must be recognizing these places.

When we're going past All Saints Church, the service is letting out, and our gran is poking a finger at the church. The husband thinks he's got it. "That's it!" he says. "She needed to be brought here on Trinity Sunday."

"Now when's Trinity Sunday?" I ask, trying to make him see sense. "It's two days away..."

Then a little old man catches sight of our granny and starts making a fast beeline for us, waving his arms and yelling "Lidochka! Lidochka!" The husband cheers up. "See, now we know her name," he says. But the old man has run up to us and no, he says, it's not Lidochka, it's some other granny.

So where are we going to drop this one off? The husband's upset again. And then Vitalik calls. "What's your deal, driving off with someone else's granny?" he wants to know. "There's this family that came for Trinity Parents' Saturday, to commemorate the old folks. They bought their granny from Daugavpils so she can plunk herself down on her home turf and shed a tear or two. And you drove right past my granny. She hadn't got to the bench yet, by reason of her being crippled in the small of the back."

The husband comes unglued. "Are you kidding me?" he says. "So, we bring this one back? Or ship her to Daugavpils?"

Now Granny's just beaming. But Vitalik says, "Fetch the one you've got back here, or the government's going to be weighing in, because this is a kidnapping. And for me, you can pick up my niece, Natashka. She's by that plane that never flies and just stands there on the square. She'll be waiting for you. And get her ma too. She'll sit herself down by the side of the road, where they sell pies."

So we brought that granny back to where we'd got her from. The cat had been waiting for her on the bench the whole time. But there was no mama and no niece, because they'd taken the bus. More room to spread out there.

BATH DAY IN SHESHURINO

On Saturdays, smoke drifts over the village. The banyas are being heated. The bitter haze, from birch or aspen, floats everywhere. The old folks have the black banyas, the ones without a chimney and just a pile of stones in the middle to serve as a stove that's heated until the stones glow red, and you mustn't go in then because the air's so bad you can't even breathe. Then they open it up, but the fumes stick around so the darn place is like a smoke-house. They get going bright and early, and that's the only way to do it. There's a teensy little window, so you can't see a thing in there, not even in broad daylight.

The oldest in the family – which would be Granddad or even Great-granddad – always gets to enjoy the first steam. And when the mystical, magical Ivan Kupala Day is coming up, in early July, he'll gather herbs to dry too, muttering his spells over them. He'll collect potentilla root, rowanberry leaves, cocklebur, the sticky catchfly that makes your fingers all gummy, and angelica root that's sweetish to the taste, and for sharpness he'll grind some juniper needles in a pestle. The women do their bit as well, for the hair-washing part of it, collecting soapwort, whose pale, whitish little flowers sort of lather when you rub them between your fingers. In the villages, people use potash to wash their hair, by sifting out the ashes and boiling up what's left. And there's your shampoo, there's your soap.

As for rinsing, well, it varies – some like to steep a birch-twig switch in the rinse water, others prefer oak. But everyone steams with burdock, because no one has ever found anything better than burdock, better than its soft leaves and beetroot-colored burrs. It's all floated in a basin, and the pale water turns brownish. And the fibrous bark is torn off linden trees and plaited, and that takes some tearing, believe you me. But then again, the work makes you sweat like mad, which is a load off the body...

The steaming is a lengthy process. Before his first steam, Granddad, with a towel wound around his hips, goes in for a moment, squinting from the fumes, to splash some strong, home-brewed beer onto the stones with a wooden scoop. That sends a hearty, yeasty, heady aroma all through the banya... In the dressing room, the women are setting out the clean linens, stacking them in even piles – this one Pa's, that one Grandpa's. Clean underpants and outer pants, side-collar shirts... Before going in, everyone wearing a cross takes it off so as not to get burned, wrapping it in a scrap of cloth and putting it somewhere safe.

The broad bench is spread with a towel, and on it is placed a jug of home-brewed kvas made with leftover rye crusts. They crush some mint to make it smell good, and scatter a little mound of sour apples, and cranberries or viburnum fruit in fall.

Then the grandpas, wearing their old hats, will go in, crossing themselves – right into the very thickest steam, into the dense cloud of aromas. They sit themselves down on the shelves in silence, except for the groaning. They endure the heat because it warms their bones all through, drives the chill from their bodies. And the first who can't stand it, he shoulders his way out the door and heads for the lake and goes straight off the jetty into the cold water, sending up great puffs of steam. The women turn aside bashfully...

The two-fisted men are next, the no-nonsense ones – the tractor operators and the lumberjacks – coming for their wash and their steam, and after that the banya always smells the same, reeking of diesel fuel and engine oil. When they leave, you have to wave a juniper switch around and pour vinegar on the little stone stove, and that's how that goes.

But what about the women? When the women get in with the little kids, there's squealing, squeaking, raucous laughter, and slaps on bare backs – stop your crying, soap's not like shame, it won't eat your eyes out! The littlest ones go into the trough to be washed first, and then the women have their time to rest. They lie on the shelves, send up a cloud of fresh steam, and work each other over with switches. The old girls lay into you mercilessly; the birch leaves stick to well-steamed bodies like mustard plasters... Our women like to spread ferns on the floor that make the banya smell like you're walking in the woods...

My neighbor Nadyukha and I go in for the last steam, trying not to touch the black, soot-smeared walls. It's already dark in there, but the stove is holding its heat and the cistern's full of hot water. Nadyukha sits her Varya on the slippery bench and rubs her scrawny little back with a washcloth until it's red and Varya's squealing. She has blond, almost flaxen, hair, and she's as proud of it as any little girl would be. Some

summer visitors have given her a lovely bottle of shampoo, and the lather fluffs up on her hair in a luxurious, frothy cap, and rainbow-tinted soap bubbles fly everywhere. She pops them between her palms and laughs. Nadyukha douses her with warm water and recites, like a spell: "Like water off a duck's back, that's how my Varya's skinniness will go. You're going to be chubby and the prettiest of them all!"

Varya snuffles and lets a tear fall, a trial tear.

"No, Grammaaa" –and the tears are streaming down now –"I don't want to be pudgy. You... Oh, you're wider than a door, can't get into your housecoat, the buttons fly off... I don't want to be like that! I'll be like a model instead, and after that I'll be walking in a fashion show. Auntie Dasha, oh, she showed me a magazine, with pictures. There was a girl in it who lived in a village too, and then she went and got gorgeous, and they gave her a modeling job. Now she lives in France, she's married to a prince, he's bought her a yacht, all sorts of beautiful rings... And a car, red as red can be, and a castle, for real, and she's started singing and now they know her everywhere... So why would I be herding cows in a village? I want the beautiful too!"

Nadyukha rinses out the basin, dunks the workaday linens in it, rubs them with soap, and says, looking over in my direction: "That Auntie Dasha of yours should read you something out of another magazine ... Oh yes ... About how there was once a featherbrain, pretty as a picture, but she married a drunk. And how she's got a tumbledown shack now and an old motorcycle instead of a red car, and wears felt boots on her bare feet. But she can still sing just as good as your model."

"But Grammaaa," Varya wails, her tears falling into the linen basin, "Auntie Dasha's husband was in the movies, and he's from the village too, and everyone went to the rec center to look at him."

"You'll never be a box-office smash," Nadyukha says with certainty, cramming Varya into a warm pair of pants. "You don't have the main thing an actress needs."

"What's that?" Varya isn't crying any more.

"You've got no butt. Without a butt, a woman doesn't count as a woman at all." She pulls on Varya's felt boots and shakes her fist at me behind the kid's back. "What were you asked to read to the child? AN ALPHABET BOOK!"

And we go out of the banya into the fresh air, where we give off the smell of birch switches and a touch of vinegar. Evening is falling...

A QUILT ON THE DOOR AND
CATS IN THE FRIDGE

After the hospital closed, Mishka Sparrowlegs' wife Nadyukha – no spring chicken but not eligible for a pension either – was out of work and therefore out of money. And her husband had been in the same boat for a while, ever since the state farm fell apart. Mishka's a welder, but what's he going to weld when there's no iron to be had? So he just lies around thinking, wondering where the money's going to come from.

Sure, a village doesn't have everything a town has, but the kitchen garden keeps on birthing potatoes and there's a piglet grunting away in what passes for a barn. Still, there's no doing without money. You figure it out. You need flour, right? Matches? Soap too, and who knows what-all else? And then there's the most important thing in a village, especially in wintertime – firewood. Without firewood, the stove won't give you the time of day, and in a Russian village, it's the stove that keeps everything going. It gives heat and cooks soup and warms water and dries socks, and on top of that it offers the cats somewhere to dream about mice. And if the snow starts flying, what could be better than clambering onto the sleeping ledge, covering up with an old fur coat, and getting some shut-eye?..

Our village doesn't have a store of its own, but a mobile store, a trailer on wheels, does come by. It carries the mail too, because what if someone writes a letter to someone else? Although that seldom happens these days: really, what's there to write about? But we do buy newspapers, and why wouldn't we? It's all spelled out in the paper – what the weather's going to be like, how many rubles there are to the dollar, when the district center's going to have chickens for sale. No, how can you do without the printed word? And then after you've read it, there's always something to wrap in it, or you can make a hat out of it... And so Nadyukha decided to buy herself a paper too. Why? Who knows – she's a woman, and a woman's a riddle. But the newspaper was passed on to me – you're cultured and all that, they said, you read.

True enough, but meanwhile, Nadyukha's coming unglued next door, yelling that someone's stolen her newspaper.

I went over to her place. Finding my way with difficulty through the kitchen garden, which was overgrown with mugwort, stepping on old basins and buckets, I finally made it to Nadyukha's hut. A good ten years ago, the door had been padded with a quilt, cover and all, to keep the drafts out in winter. By now, though, the quilt's all in tatters, from the dogs or the cats or maybe just because...

Even in the entry, it smelled of gasoline, sour kasha, rotten rags, and stale hay. Kicking the door open with my foot, I went inside. Nadyukha was sitting in the kitchen, her cheek resting on her fist, puzzling out a crossword and stumbling over every letter. "Leader?" she asked herself and wrote in uneven letters *LENIN*...

"Hey, Nad," I called to her. "What 'Lenin'? You're way behind the times."

Nadyukha yawned. "I don't know anyone else with five letters," she said.

The hut was so cold, I made for the stove... The old refrigerator – pre-Freon, from back when fridges used ammonia – was juddering like mad.

"What's that for?" I asked, leaning on the stove and nodding toward the fridge.

"Don't get smudges on you," Nadyukha warned. "It's just been whitewashed. And the cats are put up in the fridge. All four of them"

"But they'll freeze."

"Nah. It's warmer there than in the house."

"And who put them in there?"

"They're not telling," Nadyukha said, laying the pen aside. "So hand over the newspaper. Else there's nothing to fire up the stove with."

We went into the "parlor." The television was flickering in the corner; there was sound but no picture. Mishka Sparrowlegs was dozing on the sofa, under what had once been a tulle curtain. The heels of his bare feet, after a lifetime spent in blissful ignorance of socks, were black.

"He's sleeping?" I asked quietly.

"He's reading," Nadyukha said proudly. "You gave me a book the other year."

"The Solzhenitsyn you mean?" I was dumbfounded.

"D'you think he knows one from another? He can't make out the letters..."

"I sense the meaning with my heart." This came from beneath the tattered lacework. "A good writer, that. A classic. I'll be reading a long while before I understand all the depth of it. I won't even smoke it."

Cigarettes cost good money these days and there is no money, so Nadyukha's growing tobacco in the vegetable patch, and Sparrowlegs dries it by the stove, cuts it up fine with a special knife, and then rolls it in paper. Everything comes in handy for that – *The Komsomol's Truth,* and *Arguments and Facts,* and even *AIDS-Info,* a newspaper that, Nadyukha contends, is all about smutty sex.

"Hey, Dash." Sparrowlegs scratches a heel. "Think there'll be any more newspapers?"

"To read?"

"Right. About love and about... you know, nookie."

"And you'll smoke it too?"

"No!" Mishka hauled a frayed copy of *AIDS-Info* out from under the pillow. "I read it!"

"But it's... Hang on, this copy's from 2000!"

"Right!" Sparrowlegs hoisted up his big toe. "That's the whole point. I've got the theory down pat over the past sacksteen years."

"Uh-huh," Nadyukha chimed in from the kitchen. "He's just got weaker on the practice, is all."

I looked through the window. Snow was falling, in huge, white flakes. I was freezing and wanted to go home, for a nice glass of tea with raspberry jam.

"Well, I'm off," I said to Nadyukha.

"Off with you, then, if that's all you've got."

"And who's going to light the stove?" I asked from the doorway.

"Whoever freezes first," Nadyukha replied. She dragged the coverlet off Mishka, threw it around her shoulders, and went to puzzle some more over her crossword. I opened the fridge, let the crazed cats out, and headed home.

GOA AND GREENHOUSES

Gagik Gelonyan was an only child and had everything a respectable family could provide. After graduating with a major in management from the Presidential Academy, he was a runaway success in everything he did, including some things he should have actually run away from. So his doting mamma packed him off to the Institute of Technology in Israel.

All would have been good if he had graduated from that elite school and scored a job as an analyst in a bank somewhere, golden parachute and all. But no. Instead, Gagik the golden boy set off with a bunch of other equally gilded youngsters for Tibet. Then on to Goa. And after all that, once he'd found a place in his heart for the teachings of Buddhism, gone vegan, and sprouted a wondrous man-bun, he realized that being an analyst was stupid. He had to turn himself around and buck the system.

Time was, someone like that would become a roving mercenary or a pirate. Now they join an ashram or make their home out in the country. Gagik opted for the absolutely exotic step of moving to the Russian countryside. If he'd gone to an Armenian village, that would have been the end of it. After eighteen months in those high mountain pastures, he would have scuttled on down to Yerevan, had a shave, bought a high-end Italian suit, and headed back to Moscow. But a Russian village is a whole different proposition because it has diddly squat to offer. No goats, no mountains, no electricity.

Gagik thought of Chekhov, whom he'd never read, and hired on as a village school teacher.

"And what would you be, young fellow?" asked Grandpa Vanya, eyeing the bearded young loiterer outside the school. "A gypsy, I dare say?"

The young women of the village were walking by, hand in hand with children dressed to the nines, it being the First of September, the first day of school, Knowl-

edge Day. There was a lot of side-eye for the bushy-bearded fellow in a peculiar outfit of wide, high-water pants and a colorfully embroidered shirt worn untucked. And, as if that wasn't enough, he hadn't a thing on his feet.

"Lordy, what a bum!" Ninka said to Zinka. "Must have been burned out of house and home."

"Or he's a jailbird," said Zinka to Ninka. "They rob them poor devils blind in the joint. Somebody's even stolen his boots! If that don't beat all..."

While the locals went right on looking sideways at their quadrilingual prodigy, Gagik started cramming his vision of the world into his little charges' easily moldable minds. Seated at his desk, he launched into tales of his recent travels in India, and the island of Goa, and the Indian Ocean, and the sacred cows. The whole class yucked it up when informed that people there don't eat cows. Photos of the Buddha made the girls blush for some reason. And when the boys heard the word "ashram," they keeled over laughing.

The district mucky-mucks, with their Soviet-era education, weren't too thrilled about that view of the world. But there was no one to put in Gagik's place.

Not long afterward, a young biology teacher called Snezhana showed up and promptly fell in love with him, because, college educated as she was, who else did she have to love? And when you're in love, you're up for anything, so Snezhana started eating radishes. To this day, no one knows how the offbeat, not to say outlandish, Gagik captivated her, but the fruit of that captivity was a wonderful, curly-haired little boy they named Ovsep, in honor of one of Gagik's distant ancestors. It was also Gagik's way of sticking it to rural Russia.

Gagik and his significant other were aiming for minimalism in everything. But shabby clothing strategically slit to show glimpses of young bodies – that's all well and good in Goa. What the Russian countryside demands is sheepskin coats, earflap hats, and felt boots. And a hut with a stove. Gagik was bound and determined not to knuckle under to the climate of northwestern Russia, but the Russian snows had him beat there. Gagik swathed his rickety, lopsided little hut in regally luxurious style, using an advertising banner he'd found somewhere.

But family life is all about self-denial. Because a family wants food, beds, chairs, clothing, and a wardrobe for the clothes. When he'd decided on withdrawing from the world, Gagik never thought that his wife would have her mind set on sleeping in a bed. With a mattress. And, preferably, sheets.

The thoroughly dumbfounded Gagik called his mom in Haifa. International wire transfers are a breeze these days, so he got the money, duly converted into rubles, and mournfully spent it on a double bed with an innerspring mattress. He also made his peace, after some hemming and hawing, with a dozen pans, some skillets, and a set of eco-friendly plates, but he never abandoned his commitment to what some might call "living green." In the spring, following a happily snowed-in winter that could well have resulted in a little brother (or maybe sister) for Ovsep, the Gelonyans started growing vegetables.

The sight of Snezhana wandering the meager, sandy soil in a flowery sari while carrying her infant son in a knotted sling and bottle-feeding him soy milk on the go filled the neighbors with righteous horror.

"To torment the poor babe so!" the old girls wailed. "Refusing him the breast, did you ever see the like?"

Gagik's mom, unlike his dad, took her only son's needs to heart, and the money transfers came in like clockwork. When you have money, life is possible – even in the Russian countryside.

The villagers were as astounded by the novelties on Gagik's property as Russia's serfs had been at their first sight of a steam-powered threshing machine. Well furnished with theory, and hungry too, he somehow managed to grow things that had never been grown in the village before. Arugula sent up its fresh, green spikes; purple basil glistened; planters were dark with eggplants; and bizarrely colored tomatoes dangled like bunches of grapes. And there were grapes ripening too. Water recirculating around the greenhouses warmed the soil, while cunning little devices kept track of temperature and moisture, and even flashed the chemical composition of the soil on a display.

Wanting nothing to do with animal carcasses, the Gelonyans extracted their proteins and minerals from the treasure trove that is the World Wide Web. The bulgur, couscous, garbanzo beans, lentils, pecans, cashews, and other vegan delights came by mail, puzzling the post office mice, who were used to a very different diet.

The deeper the Gelonyans delved into raw foods, the greater the distance they put between themselves and the other villagers. They couldn't bear the sight of anyone eating a sausage. Still, the seclusion was good for them. Roe deer came right up to their house. Hawks flew overhead, disappointed not to see the standard-issue chickens down below. Bears grunted in the forest. And foxes barked.

But alas! Happiness sometimes comes to a sudden end. Gagik's mom married for the third time and went off to Australia. Husband Number Three, a horrendous tightwad, slapped a veto on sending any more financial support to her son, for the simple reason that it's not how things are done around here. The kid's thirty; let him go get a job.

Gagik would actually have liked to, but there wasn't a job to be had anywhere in the village.

When the money stopped, so did the electricity. The Mercedes G-class ran out of gas, and the cunning little displays went dark. Gagik and Snezhana had to haul water from the well, eat nettle flatbreads, and drink fireweed tea. The packages weren't arriving anymore; the proteins and the carbs ran out. Snezhana's saris were threadbare, and Gagik's beard reached down to his knees. Sensing his illusions collapsing around him, Gagik left Snezhana and Ovsep to tend the vegetables, while he up and vanished. Because the Buddha's ideals are attainable anywhere, even in Moscow.

Snezhana built a bonfire to burn her saris, tucked Ovsep under her arm, nailed up the house, and headed for the district center. Where she taught secondary-school biology. But to this day, the villagers still find tiny, unripe melons in the ruins of the greenhouses.

LIFE IS JUST A BOWL OF... BERRIES?

Mid-July came on chilly and with rain to spare, but month's end was suddenly dry and warm. That gave the wild raspberries, which usually ripened in early August, an unexpected influx of the mysteriously delicate juice that make them so very different from the fragrant but bland garden raspberries. So the gals, without so much as a word to each other, started making forays into the closest of the raspberry patches that in the past couple of years had run riot over the felled areas of the forest. After the nearest mile or two had been picked clean, they put their heads together and started going in threes, in fives, because the forest won't put up with any tomfoolery.

Only Granny Shura, a cantankerous old biddy with a sharp, spiky tongue that made her nobody's favorite, still went out alone, for both the raspberries and the wild herbs that should only be gathered after Ivan Kupala Day. With her old-school ways, she didn't hold with frivolous attire. She also didn't think much of mosquitoes, so she swaddled herself up, with a sweater jacket over a flannel shirt and on top of that, a canvas raincoat when it was threatening rain, all of which made her look like something between a mossy hillock and a fir tree withered from the roots up.

The young lasses, both married and single, roamed around the raspberry patches in a cheerful, garish flock, wearing light, gaudy sundresses and eye-popping headscarves that butterflies would settle on. But then there were the rubber boots, always the rubber boots, and that was nothing to laugh at, what with the marshy soil over here and the slithery snakes over there. They scattered across the cleared spots like a merry flight of birds, roaring with laughter and yelling to each other, or they'd suddenly strike up a song – all at once, without a word spoken – and it was always about love gone dismally wrong.

The raspberry baskets were willow or bast, with an open weave so the berries wouldn't get squashed. The girls would brace the canes against their fronts and with

quick fingers strip the berries, trying to not to let any that were overripe, or crushed, or had a beetle along for the ride get into their baskets. The gorgeous Nyurka, the village's number one cut-up, could pop a berry in her mouth and needle the girl next to her and sing along all at the same time.

And on they pressed, because the berries seemed bigger and juicier the deeper in they went, plus they could grab up a few of the cloudberries that trailed over the mossy mounds, and blackberries too, still unripe by July and puckery in the mouth. They gradually wandered farther away from each other, hallooing back and forth, quietly at first and then less often, and only when one of them was all alone by a raspberry patch that bordered on a dense thicket, when the wind was bending the pine branches overhead, did the desperate wailing begin: "N-i-i-i-nka? Mashka! Mashka! Nyurka! Have you seen Valentina? No? Stay still, Mash, I'm coming your way. Stay still, I can't see a blessed thing!"

The raspberry patches were interspersed with small marshes, deceptively green, as if someone had spread a plush rug underfoot. But if you step on it, there's a squelching sound and a second later, that sucking feeling, and you'll be lucky if you just lose a boot, because there have been times when a gal went into the forest and never came back.

But this time everything went off just fine, and they sat down in a glade, under a nut tree, and unfolded fresh-laundered kitchen towels and set out their simple fare of boiled eggs, rye bread, cheese home made from eggs stewed with milk curds, and young green onions too. And a rag-plugged bottle put in an appearance, as usual – a bottle of murky moonshine brewed from blackcurrant buds. They drank daintily, a sip at a time, nibbling on eggs and onions and washing it down with water drawn from a nearby brook as cheery as it was tiny.

"A pretty sight, girls," said Mashka, lying back. "See how heavy this nut tree's crop'll be. Will we be here come fall?"

"That we will," Ninka yawned. "Why wouldn't we? The summer folk'll shell out a tenner for a glassful of them nuts on the market."

"And what about cranberry season?" Lolling back against a pine tree, Valentina, the oldest, ruffled a cowberry bush with her hand. "First there's the cowberry, then there's the bilberry, but you'd better not miss the cranberries, or else the folk from Kropilino and Lokhi will swoop in and leave the place bare."

"Right you are," the other girls chimed in. "Cranberries fetch a much better price."

The sun had peeped out, making drowsy heads nod, and they fell asleep any old way, some seated and others on their sides. And that, wouldn't you know it, was exactly when Granny Shura, bundled up like a haystack, came waddling out, ten yards or so away, into her favorite forest tract, griping under her breath about these floozies from who-knows-where who'd looted everything and couldn't stay put at home while she, and at her age too, had to clamber through places like this where you could break every leg you've got.

But to any outside observer, the source of that muffled grumbling couldn't possibly have been a person, because then you'd have been able to make out the words. But no, not this time. Some kind of animal was coming their way, trampling through the bushes, and the dry brush was crackling, and the creature was snorting.

Mashka was the first to wake. A summer snooze in the heat of the day, after a few slugs of moonshine – no telling what dreams that'll bring.

"Oh, mother of mine!" Mashka wailed. "Oh, my dear, my darling girls! The horror! Oh, drat and darn!"

Valentina unglued her swollen eyes. "Why're you hollering like a stuck pig?" she asked. "Seen the devil, have you? Or just a tractor driver?"

And then...

"BAAAAAR!" – it was a blood-curdling roar – "Girls! Run for your lives! Frickety frack, oh my, oh my! I've been hearing how a summer visitor, she got mauled this very year!"

That last part she had to yell at their backs, because they'd

bolted in every direction, lumbering as they ran because our lasses are no lightweights. In fact, they're chunky. Because what's the good of being all skin and bones here in the village?

And so they ran – or, rather, galloped – jumping over wind-felled trees, the baskets tied to their belts scattering raspberries all the way.

Valentina got completely stuck between two pines and couldn't so much as budge. She was roaring like a halfwit, she was crying. But all that Granny Shura could hear, being deaf to start off with and wearing a headscarf too, was "Bear, bear!" Scared to death, she took off after the lasses, to catch up with them and save herself. What they saw, though, was a hulking great animal, maybe gray, maybe brown, that seemed to be standing on its hind legs and roaring too, which meant it had to be a she-bear. And what if, God forbid, there was a cub somewhere close? That was as bad as it gets.

On they flew, to the logging station, with the lasses in front and Granny Shura behind, until she got tangled up in some bushes and took to howling and moaning.

The loggers were sitting on a length of timber for an after-lunch smoke, and when they saw all this, they collapsed in helpless laughter. "On a cross-country sprint are you, lasses?" they wanted to know. "Then you should at least be wearing striped shorts and tank tops, 'cos that's not a sporty look at all."

The lasses pulled up short, their arms and legs scratched and stuck all over. This one had shed her boot, that one had torn her skirt.

"Bear!" they said when they'd caught their breath. "Yonder. It's been charging at us all the way from Site Four! You'd best run and get a rifle."

"And who're we going to shoot?" the men guffawed. "Granny Shura? Nah, nothing short of an aspen spike through the heart'll be the death of her."

The lasses turned around, and there it was – a shapeless canvas sack lying in a bramble thicket and wheezing. They came down hard on Granny Shura for scaring them, and rightly so. But now they take her with them on their raspberry hunts, because she knows the secret places. Instead of a canvas coat, though, they make her wear an orange vest. With reflectors.

THE THIMBLE

Pashka Bystrov, known around the village as Speedy, was leaning back against the warm stove and despondently watching his wife, Galka. Her hair still in curlers, she was tossing her dresses, skirts, and fleece tights into a suitcase, wadding up her feather-light stockings, and yelling at him that she was sick up to here, and then some, with village life, and she wanted to hear her heels tapping on asphalt and get a proper salon perm. Pashka had no arguments against any of that, so he just smoked, sending soft, grayish circles up toward the ceiling. When the door slammed shut behind her, Pashka felt a sudden surge of the rage that had been burning him up inside for months now, hauled off, and smashed a fist into the wedding photograph that hung on the wall, framed behind glass. Then, licking the blood from his fingers, Pashka groped around in the cellar for a bottle, wrenched out the cork, and drank the whole thing without bothering about a glass. And promptly fell asleep.

The state farm that went bust a couple of years earlier had allotted plots of land to the workers, but that land was worthless, impossible to plow, more bogs and gullies than anything else. And selling it would bring in a pittance, at best.

Everyone who was able to scattered, to the towns and the cities, but those who as children had fallen heart and soul for the dense stands of pine and the pristine little river, who couldn't have hacked it in a human anthill – they stayed in the village, to live out their days there. And somehow they slogged through it. Whoever could still muster the strength did the traditional potato planting around May Day, brined their cabbages in fall, drove the web-footed gray geese to the pond, and kept empty-headed, bleating sheep, although there'd long been no call for their wool. Then all of a sudden outsiders came, quickly set up a logging operation, hired guys for hilariously stingy wages, and again life flowed on. Not exactly a river of life, but... well, a rivulet at least.

Being a technically minded fellow, Pashka was brought on to drive a skidder tractor, and the wages weren't bad, so the only bad thing was that Pashka was being eaten up with yearning. When the state farm's property was portioned out, Pashka got a lousy little tractor, which he fixed up, and now he'd plow the old girls' household plots so they could plant their potatoes or he'd shove snow off the road in winter. A tractor driver's always held in high honor, because he can haul manure to the fields or take some
old thing on her last journey.

Pashka did let his hut go, though. And well he might, because where's he supposed to wash and rinse the curtains? When's he supposed to swing a broom after a hard day's work? So the spiders had come crawling in and made themselves at home in the corners, and a mouse had gnawed at Granddad's chest of drawers, and the general air of neglect grated worse than sandpaper on Pashka's soul.

Aside from Pashka, there was almost no one left in the village, only Granny Zhenya, his next-door neighbor, and Grandpa Stepanych, and he lived out by the forest. But one day – a day off, it was – a car rumbled up, and doors slammed, and he heard something resembling voices. He looked out, and in a neighbor's yard stood a young woman, dressed like a townie and surrounded by bundles and suitcases. The local ragamuffins were scooting around, and a dog was barking. Pashka hollered from his porch (joking, like), "Hey-ho, neighbor, I don't seem to know your face. Who would you be?" But she turned around and said, "Really, Pash, you don't know your own people?"

It was Lenka, Granny Sima's granddaughter. Old Sima had died long before, and Pashka hadn't seen hide nor hair of Lenka since the wake. A puny little thing she'd been back then, just a chit of a girl. Huge eyes, skinny as a rake, and more trouble than a grandma's nanny goat. But look at her now, the beauty she was, with that well-turned figure. She really had it all, and her eyes were just the same. Pashka put two and two together and made four. She'd lived awhile in town and had a son, but it didn't work out, so she's back. But what for?

Pashka swept her a low, joking bow and went back inside, to his sofa. He turned on the television. It was an American movie, with shooting, lots of bloodshed, and people behaving badly – something nice to fall asleep to. And when he woke, it was morning, early and gray. He did the usual, rattling the bucket down the well, giving the chickens their feed, having a quick shave, and gulping down his tea with a hunk of bread and a wedge of cheap sausage before heading off to work. But all day long, he couldn't get that Lenka off his mind. She'd grown up pretty enough to make his heart quiver whenever he thought of her.

And that's when the one-sided staring contests started. He'd see Lenka stacking wood, and he'd go up and shoulder her out of the way. Let me, he'd say, it's no big deal. And he'd haul so much water for her that she had to go out at night and drain half the barrel. In spring he took his tractor to dig up the potato trenches – and nearly screwed his head off, watching Lenka sort the potatoes into buckets. And that kid of hers, little Igor, was smart and savvy. Pashka even gave him tractor rides and took him out to the hayfield, because why not? The boy needed to get used to all that.

So it went on, for about a year. At one point, Lenka and her son left to see their folks for a week, and Pashka stopped sleeping, plain and simple. He was forever finding a way to just happen to be out on the road. I'm taking a walk, he'd say, don't mind me. But actually he was gazing out toward the highway. And his pals would want him to go fishing, and his granddad would call about making a visit to the banya and having a drink or two. But he never went anywhere; it was all he could do to get himself to work. Then when Lenka came back, when he saw her, he nearly ran his tractor into a fence.

"Pash," Lenka said between peals of laughter, "Why're you so red? Fresh from the banya, are you? Or did you get too much sun?"

Pashka grumbled something in reply, ducked into his house, and beelined it to the sofa. He plastered himself to the wall and said to himself, "I love her. That's what it is. No way I can live without her." Then he stood up, splashed his face with water at the sink, combed his hair into a side part, and went to her place. To talk.

She opened the door but didn't ask him in, just stood there with a look that said "Now what?" And he was so agitated, all his words clumped together and stuck in his throat, and he couldn't say hey, yay, or nay. He stood there for a while, gave up, and left. The whole winter he'd gawk at her from behind the curtains, but at night he'd clear the snow from her pathways, chop kindling for her – and was afraid to show his face.

Then spring came. It was March 8, Women's Day, no sooner, no later. At work, Pashka and the other guys congratulated the women, drank sickly sweet wine, and gave them each a bunch of wilted tulips. And Granny Klava whispered into Pashka's ear, "Have you fallen in love, my boy?"

Pashka thumped himself in the chest. "Who?" he asked. "Me? What would I want with that? I'm footloose and fancy-free…"

"No you're not," Granny Klava said. "I can see somebody's caught that fancy of yours. You're all shriveled up with love. You should go a-courting, dearie, and be done with it. Such a girl she is! A blazing fire! If one of the summer people whisks her away, you'll be kicking yourself. Buy her a ring, get down on one knee, and say, 'Here, Lena, take my hand and my heart!' And that'll be that."

"Now where am I going to find a ring?" the dumbfounded Pashka wanted to know. "The stores are closed."

"This'll do you," said Granny Klava, giving him a thimble. "Give her this for now."

Pashka turned the little cap-shaped thing around and around. "But it's a thimble," he said. "Where's she going to put it?"

"On her finger, that's where!" Klava was what passed for a wise woman in those parts. "You'd think a thimble goes on your thumble, but it don't. It goes on your finger, so it's nearly a ring."

And Pashka was off like a shot. But evening had come, the ice had started breaking up, so he was slipping and sliding. Still, he ran all the way to Lenka's house, and then what? Yell? He'd wake everyone up. So he decided to throw snowballs. At the wall. But one veered off, toward the door, and that was exactly when Lenka opened up, so she got it square on the forehead.

"What d'you think you're doing, you hoodlum?" a furious Lenka wanted to know. "A grown man, and can't stop acting the fool!"

Pashka went up to her, put the thimble on her finger, and said, "Marry me. I'll be little Igor's pa."

Lenka tore the thimble from her finger, flung it away so hard it jingled when it landed, and said, "So I can darn your socks? Oh, joy!"

And *bang* went the door. Then she locked it.

Pashka shuffled back to his hut and was again gripped with such yearning, such pain, that he guzzled a good half-bucketful of chilled vodka, fell back onto the sofa, and howled at the very top of his lungs. But while he was staring at the wall, he didn't see Lenka, bundled up in a jacket, wandering around her yard with a flashlight. She was looking for the thimble. When she came back in, her son asked, "Did you lose something, Ma?"

"Uh-huh," said Lenka. "My happiness."

HOOK, LINE, AND SINKER

The young scallywags of Sheshurino and Nagovye would fish in a stream that linked Lake Nagovye with its forest tributaries. There was a pier with skinny little cross-beams, where the junior contingent perched on the planks, bare legs dangling, and their elders stood at the rail, shelling sunflower seeds and spitting the hulls into the water. Inquisitive little ruffes would swim up to the odor of sunflower and circle around, grabbing onto the worm while they were there, drowning it once and for all, giving it a good gnawing, and then, to the fishermen's great vexation, sneaking away from the hook. Poles cut from a hazelnut tree, line pilfered from Dad or Granddad, homemade floats, and rusty hooks were the sum total of the fishing tackle. They dumped the small fry into a shared bucket, while the neighborhood cats sat demurely, waiting for lunch.

A car pulled up at the pier. This pipsqueak of a guy got out, reached into the gaping maw of his trunk, and started unloading onto the road small cases, rod tubes, boxes, a folding chair, a little spirit stove, a tea kettle, a plastic table, and other odds and ends that gave off a delicious whiff of foreign lands. Open-mouthed, the scallywags watched as he put on a new pair of hip boots and a life vest the color of rotting greenery, and assembled his fishing rod. As section was mated to section, the rod opened out like a telescope, eventually reaching its maximum length. Then the guy started pulling out lures as shiny as ladies' earrings, bait that looked disgusting but smelled great, floats, and, to top it all off, a sonar fish finder. The scallywags turned their backs on the bucket with its plashing fish to keep an eye on him.

"OK, you dimwitted rubes, see how fishing is done!" he said and flourished his rod. Its far end whooshed up and short-circuited an overhead power line, there was a cheerful crackle, and the little guy was knocked on his butt. The scallywags turned away and went back to throwing bread crumbs and spitting seed hulls into the water...

And here's one that fairly boggles the mind. One time, a fisherman came along, bringing kids with him. A bunch of them, in all shapes and sizes, little 'uns and bigger 'uns. And what d'you expect from a fisherman? He had his worms, his nets, his lures, and watching those kids was the last thing on his mind. The upshot of it was that one of the girls – not a tiny one but not a well-grown one either, more of a neither-here-nor-there – got sick. I was in a flap, too scared to take her temperature. She was just burning up. "Oh good grief!" thinks I. "Either she has to have some sort of meddercation or she needs to be taken straight to Toropets." I was so agitated, I had already got into the boat. And then the fishermen come sailing in.

"It's real bad!" I holler. "SOS! We've got to go to town! Or boil some syringes… Get hot jars so we can give her a cupping…"

But he's just sitting there, still as the scales on a fish. Silent. Calm.

"My dear lady," says he, "you're having a big, noisy panic and for no good reason. There's no need for any kind of treatment. We'll have it all fixed in a jiffy."

And he pulls a whole stick of summer sausage out of his cooler.

"Yikes, pops!" I say. "Are you going to beat on her?"

No, he wasn't. He handed the sausage to the kid, and she whittled on it, up one side and down the other, and the thermometer hissed and iced right over. Fell all the way to 95 degrees. And that was that: wonders'll never cease.

Their poppa explained it like this: "Here's the thing – everybody brings a first aid kit with them. I bring a sausage. The kid has a deficiency. A sausage deficiency."

There's just no telling the illnesses you'll come across these days…

LYONUSHKA AND RUBLE BILL

There was a girl called Lyonushka who lived in our village. She was of average height but nicely put together. Her hair was blonde, flaxen-blonde – bleached flax, that is, and the Russian word for "bleached" is *belyony*, so Lyonushka was a name that fit her perfectly. And she had beautiful eyes, cool as river water. She was an odd one, though – more of a spectacle than a miracle. A lot of people thought she was no better than a half-wit.

She'd collect all sorts of sick critters. Folks would bring her this, that, and the other – a squirrel, a hedgehog, and as for the cats... They needed drowning, but the womenfolk felt sorry for them and dumped them on Lyonushka, to her great delight. She fed the wee ones milk through the nipple of a baby bottle, and collected herbs out in the forest and brewed them up for the sick ones to drink. Even a little bird with a broken wing – she'd bind it up and make it well. So after that, the birds would fly and fly around her home.

Kolya the stable boy was courting Lyonushka. Hale and hearty he was, curly haired and broad shouldered. The girls were like to die for love of him. But Kolya and Lyonushka became an item. They'd often go to the social club of an evening. He'd have her by the elbow and she'd be cracking sunflower seeds all the while, showing off her white teeth. And laughing her head off. She was a cheerful one.

And didn't he love her!.. She'd be out working on the farm, and he'd go to meet her, take her something for lunch. And he fixed up her hut, kept everything in great shape. He was good with his hands, that one. And there she'd be, laughing it up.

Now one time – it was closing in on International Women's Day – he decided to buy her a present, so she'd have something like a dowry. He saved up his money, put it inside a book. And he went to the district department store and bought her a set of dishes. The real thing, imported from Germany and unbelievably beautiful. The little plates and the soup tureen had these sheaves of rye grass braided with poppies and

ga

all wound around with golden ribbons... People from the village had been going all that way just to admire it. So expensive it was as well: two hundred and twenty rubles. So he bought it, they put it all into a box for him, pinging each plate with a pencil to make sure none of them were cracked. And they tied it up with a ribbon.

Kolya only had a beer or two, not a drop more. Then he caught the evening bus, which was packed. He found himself a place in back, put the box on his knees... and nodded off... But the bus went over a bump on Crooked Hill, and the box fell. Right onto the floor. Kolya woke up and oh, no, no, no... Everybody came over to help, untied the ribbon ... and there it was, all that beauty smashed to bits. He's sitting there nearly in tears and just about ready to put himself out of his misery. But the peasant woman sitting next to him asks, "Haven't you *any* money left for a present, dearie?" Kolya shows her a ruble, meaning that's all there is. And the woman hands him... a piglet. She hadn't managed to sell this one, this runty little leftover. Kolya was so heartsick, he took it – because he couldn't go and propose with empty hands, could he?

Here to this day we revere the good order that our grandfathers put in place, so it's a formal proposal or nothing at all. Marriages would be registered at the village soviet (because hardly anybody went to church), but matchmakers still had to be sent. Kolya goes to his friends Petya and Vanya, asking them to be his matchmakers at Lyonushka's, to ask her to marry him. But they're snickering up their sleeves,

wanting to know if he's been stuffing himself with the henbane that makes you crazy, or worse. "Why the hell would she have you, such a looker as she is?" they ask. "Go have your fun," they say, "'cos you'd be nuts to put a ring on it. Besides, she's such a whack job, you'll think you're living in a zoo." So they wanted nothing to do with it.

The village had a school, though, built by the master back in the day, and it had an old teacher who'd taught both Lyonushka and Kolya. And Kolya falls at his feet and begs him for help, saying something like, "I need to show my Lyonushka respect and love, but everybody's laughing at me, and nobody'll be my matchmaker."

"What's not to respect?" the old teacher said. "So much love, and you're a good lad, and our Lyonushka's an angel, pure and simple."

All her life, Lyonushka had had no one but an unmarried aunt, a real old battleax inside and out, an enemy to all mankind. She was glad to be getting Lyonushka off her hands. Kolya was a hard worker, didn't drink much, and made good money, and he'd put his foot down with Lyonushka about dragging all sorts of worthless critters into the hut. So the teacher came with Kolya – in the evening, to avoid the evil eye – and brought wine and cookies. When the aunt saw all this, she nearly lost it, because she didn't know what to use for blessing the young couple. There wasn't an icon in the house.

They enter the hut, and the aunt says, by the book, "Why have you come?" And the teacher tells her, "You have the merchandise, we have the merchant. You have the flower, we have the vase." And he shoves Kolya forward. But a bride price had to be given – money, or a length of fabric, or something else that we hold dear. And that harpy of an aunt plants her hands on her hips. She'd caught wind of the dish set, you see, so she asks straight out, "Then you've brought a piece of dress fabric or a fur coat, have you, Kolya? Or some kind of pretty dinnerware to put in the china closet?" Meanwhile, there's a piglet grunting in the sack that Kolya's holding.

"Here's the bride price," he says. "Auntie, I'll give you a piglet for my Lyonushka, to soften your temper."

The aunt cheers right up because at least he's brought something useful, but for appearance's sake, she sputters, "You're more of a downright imbecile than Lyonushka! Instead of bringing a dish set, you're pulling this swinish trick on us?"

Kolya's standing there red faced, with no eyes for anyone but Lyonushka, and she's laughing it up to herself and winking, as if to say, "Don't be scared. What kind of dowry do I come with? Cats and songbirds and not another thing."

The aunt gave her consent. There was no icon, but the teacher had brought a picture from the school, of some writer with a beard. They waved the picture around, with Kolya and Lyonushka kneeling, all right and proper. "God willing, good fortune be yours," they said.

After Kolya left, the aunt's still grumbling, but Lyonushka says to her, "If Kolya has such a soft spot for me, I'll be fine when we're married. He has a kind heart."

The wedding wasn't long in coming. The way out of the village was blocked off by young lads and girls holding hands, linking arms, and singing songs. That's what we call "shutting up the road," and it's an ancient custom. When a car came by, a ransom would have to be paid, in candy or wine, and some people would even give money. It being a folkway, the bosses didn't say we couldn't. Once the young couple has entered the hut, somebody brings them a fancy round loaf on a linen towel, and whoever takes the biggest bite of it is going to be the head of that household. The aunt got a new padlock out of her pocket, turned the key in it, and threw the key into the well, to keep the marriage strong. And then, the singing! They'd been married, as was our way, on October 14, the old feast-day in honor of the Mother of God.

Next, everyone sat down to eat. Lyonushka had made little pancakes – with honey, no less – and her aunt had sprung for a chicken. There were boiled potatoes, pickled cucumbers, and brined mushrooms, and the wine on the table was sweet, with bubbles. They partied for two days. Only Lyonushka kept jumping up from the table and running off to doctor that lost cause out there, giving it food and drink from a nipple bottle. The guests were complaining that their wine was bitter and yelling for the happy couple to kiss and sweeten it, and meanwhile the bride was in the pigsty. Still, darned if she didn't pull it through! And she called it Ruble Bill, yes she did.

They never did slaughter that little boar – Kolya wasn't having any of that. So it sits in the sty to this very day, and it's all gray and grizzled by now.

AN OLD MAN AND HIS DOG

Grandpa Sasha Panteleyev was sitting, numb with cold, on his glass-screened porch in the early evening chill, gloomily watching the flies butting stubbornly against the grimy panes as he traced a finger over paisley-patterned oilcloth and felt just terrible. Even out here, he could hear the voices of his children – Vitya the eldest, Ninka, the middle one, and Vova, the youngest – rattling on back in the house. They'd come together to mark the forty days since the death of their mother, who had passed away in a quiet hurry, as if remaining ever true to her lifelong way of not being a bother to anyone. She'd leaned over to drop the bucket into the well and stiffened like that, then she keeled over sideways and seemed to fall asleep. It was an hour before Grandpa Sasha noticed she wasn't there; he thought she'd gone to clean up around the cow, or collect the eggs, or swap nonsense with the neighbor woman over the fence, or soak the linens to be laundered, or do any of the simple everyday things that in the countryside aren't even considered work.

The whole village mourned Grandma Valya, and they carried her coffin themselves instead of loading it onto a truck, like all the others. After his wife's death, Grandpa Sasha became strangely distracted and kept thinking that he was still little, a towheaded kid running to the river in knee-length trousers and a shirt sewn from his father's army smock, carrying a hazelwood pole and a big can that had once held American hardtack and had been made over into a fishing pail. Or he was off to school, in a jacket his grandmother had knitted that embarrassed him horribly, so he pulled it off behind the granary near the school and then ran at breakneck speed, his teeth chattering from the cold. Or he was a tractor driver, and the hot sun was full in his eyes, and the tractor was rumbling and laboring, pulling a harrow behind, and, with his bangs flopping over his forehead and a cheap cigarette glued to the corner of his mouth, he tried to spot Valya among all the girls in her work crew. Or, in a new jacket and holding an accordion with a patent-leather strap, he was sitting in the back of a truck on his way to court Valya and went flying out of the truck bed into the muddy runoff from the farm...

And he carried on picturing himself this way and that, both old and young, and now he's meeting Valya and his firstborn at the district maternity hospital, and now three-year-old Vitya has cut his finger on an ax, and the blood's gushing out, and Sasha puts his lips to the wound and tries so hard to make it stop, and now Ninka, the middle one, is running to him out on the hayfield with the first jar of strawberries she's ever picked, and she trips, and the strawberries scatter across the stubble, and Ninka's crying, but Sasha gathers them carefully, so as not to crush them, and feeds them to her out of his hand, and now Vova, the youngest, has got wasted on moonshine for the first time, in the sixth grade, and Sasha takes Valya's belt and gives him a good thrashing, along with an earful of hair-raising language.

All of this filled his days, while the whole of his usual life went missing. Everything else was needless to him, because the one and only important thing was his memory of Valya, with whom he'd lived for nigh on half a century and with whom his soul had grown together as two tree trunks grow together and intertwine. So strong was the yearning for his wife that Sasha felt no desire to eat or drink. All he wanted was to sit and smoke and watch the clouds rising from his cigarette and catch a glimpse of his darling Valya.

There was a loud thud on the other side of the wall. Vitya, the eldest, said something in his deep bass, and Ninka joined in, her voice shrill and grating, like when a file is used to spread a saw's teeth. Then everything went quiet again. A door opened behind him, letting out a whiff of stove fumes, the reek of bad booze, and the rancid stink of musty rags, and Vova, the youngest, came out onto the porch. Nimble and swarthy he was, resembling neither his mother nor his father. The Leftovers is what Valya's mother used to call him.

"Well, then, Pa – made up your mind?" Vova blurted from the doorway, at his father's back. "Come on, now, sign the papers. We'll set you up in an apartment in town, if you don't want to stay with us, and there you'll live your life. Until," he sniggered, "you die. Pa, come on, while there's still a buyer for the house. They've already forked over the deposit, Pa. Why won't you do this friendly, like?"

Vova came close to his father and whispered into his shirt collar, which covered a neck tanned by the summer sun. "Do it, Pa... Else we'll put you in an old folks' home so you can while away your days with the gimps, and how'd that be, eh?"

Grandpa Sasha wanted to do what he did when Vova was a youngster – grab him by the forelock or by his slippery, dumpling-like ear and work him over until he wised up, the brat. But Vova had always been like this, ever since he was a little tyke, and he'd even ended up – as well they should, folks like him – joining the police force.

Then the other two came out, the chunky, bald Vitya, with his pot belly and his pricey city clothes, and Ninka, a single mother with a drinker's sly yet haggard face and Valya's kind eyes. The three of them crowded around him with their "Sell" and their "Sign," putting the scare into him, then promising him the world, then giving him the willies over the old folks' home or, worse yet, a life on the streets.

And because they were wearing on him so, and he didn't have the strength to argue anymore, he stood up, slung his quilted jacket, warm after he'd sat for so long, over his shoulders, knocked Vova's heavy hand from one of those shoulders, and went down into the yard. He unchained his dog, Gavryusha, old and weak-eyed as he was and covered in long, matted fur, and walked and walked, picking up speed, through the thinning, hazy, scarlet-leaved aspen grove, past the marsh, skillfully skirting the water holes, shuffling over the damp moss on feet familiar with these parts. And he came out onto a hillock that gave a good view for many miles around. The more distant forest formed a dense, violet crest, while closer it glowed red, sparkling in every shade of gold, and it rustled, primped, and preened, and the sun, which had shone triumphantly all day, sank westward, as if closing behind it the door to a bright and radiant world.

Sasha sat down by a pine tree split by a lightning bolt, rubbed the back of his head against its shaggy bark, let his eyelids close, and saw Valya, in a bright, citified raincoat and rubber boots. Wrapped in a fashionable scarf with "Paris" written on it, she was beaming at him merrily, and the basket of mushrooms she was holding rocked like a boat, and mushrooms fell out.

"Sasha," she yelled. "Come to me. There's such a lot of mushrooms here!"

And he lunged forward and was suddenly afraid because he was wearing an old quilted jacket, and it was awkward to be dressed like this for her to see, so young and smartly turned out as she was, but still she beckoned and called him – "Sasha, Sasha" – and he got up and ran, and she came toward him, except there was no way he could get to her. And Grandpa Sasha fell face-first into the gray moss sprinkled with rusty-colored pine needles, grasping only a handful of earth mixed with needles and tiny mushrooms. His loyal Gavryusha howled, raked the ground with his blunted claws, and lay down alongside, as if wanting to breathe warmth over the old man as he slowly froze.

READING FORTUNES

When they turn the electricity off here in the village, everybody promptly shows up at Granny Shura's. Because it's so boring, sitting at home with no light. Granny has many a tale to tell, and she knows lots of sassy little ditties and funny jokes. The girls plump themselves down to knit socks, while Granny's at her wheel, spinning her wool and telling her stories. The girls are laughing their heads off; the samovar's steaming; there are little poppy-seed bread rings and gooseberry jam on the table. So there they sit, swigging tea. The candlelight sways, and the darkness lurks in the corners, so scary. Meanwhile, though, Granny Shura always has plenty to say.

"There now, you Natashkas, Lenkas, and Lyubkas," she tells them. "You lot know nothing about life. A bunch of airheads, *and* you go shopping for a fiancé in the newspapers. What's he like, in the paper? He promises you the moon and the stars, he's a looker, doesn't drink, doesn't smoke, got all the money you could wish for, but how's it come out? Psssht! What an eyesore! He looks a fright, and he drinks like a fish, and all he's got in his pockets is moths."

"But Granny Shura, how can you find out if he's lying?" asks Natashka, who's divorced already but is still young, with white teeth, a braid down to her hind end, and a fresh-faced complexion.

Granny Shura breaks off a piece of one of her little bread rings and dips it in the jam. "Fortune-telling's what you need," she says. "You have to figure him out before you even meet. The old folks knew what they were doing. They didn't just throw themselves into it like dummies. They'd go, they'd find things out, and they'd wait. Cross-eyed but rich, or good-looking, with a forelock like Yesenin, but poor."

"And can't we have everything at once?" That's Lyubka, the youngest. Still in the homely stage of youth, her body has yet to fill out where it needs to, and she's as boney as can be, to her mother's dismay. "How about good-looking, and rich, and not a drinker?"

"Go watch a movie at the club for that." Granny Shura waddles over to the sideboard for her bottle of fruit brandy. "In life, you get one out of three."

They all have some brandy that brings the color to their cheeks, and then they start pestering Granny Shura with their "Let's tell fortunes, c'mon, let's do it."

"I know!" Lenka runs into the entryway and brings back one of her felt boots. "You have to throw this from the porch. And whichever way the toe points, that's where your fiancé's going to come from. I need for mine to point toward Moscow. Where is Moscow, anyway?"

"It's a long train ride away," says Granny Shura. "And first you have to get a ride to the train. And then you go by bus. What d'you want – to have your boot give you a taxi ride all the way there?"

"Oh, right. Or you can go to a crossroads, and the first person you run into there, you ask him his name, and that'll be your fiancé's name."

Natashka pours herself another glass. "Oh, don't make me laugh! These days, there's nobody roaming the roads except Grandpa Nikifor. And where are you going to find a Nikifor in Moscow? And what if it's a gal who comes by?"

"Oh, well, I don't know. We could read cards, then?"

"If you want, I'll let you in on an ancient kind of fortune-telling." Granny Shura wipes her fingers, which are slippery from the sheep's wool, and runs her palm over the tablecloth. "You can go to a banya. But it has to be on the dot of midnight. You won't be spooked, will you?"

"To a banya? Oh, but not the one in the forest!" Lyubka wants to get married so bad. Her ma nags the life out of her, and there's no money, and there's the cow to be milked, and the hay to mow, and she's all set to waste away, a sad old spinster, while other folks are abroad somewhere, lying on a beach. "Let's go, girls, shall we? And what then – are we going there to bathe?"

"No." Granny Shura puts a greasy deck of cards on the table and spreads them out. She's not looking for the king of diamonds but for the king of hearts, the marriage card. "We'll go to Grandpa's banya, on the village outskirts. And in the anteroom, you have to bare something, whatever you're brave enough to show: bosom or backside."

"And why's that?" Natasha's actually blushing. "What if somebody pinches us?"

"That's just it! That's what the fortune-telling's all about. You need to whisper the words and wait. If you're pinched with a smooth hand, your husband'll be a trouble maker and a skirt chaser. If you feel a stroking, he'll love you. If it's a rough hand, he'll be a mean drunk. A crippled hand means he's a pauper. If there's a bruise left on you, he'll be a thug. And if there's something like a coin stuck on the bare spot, he's rich."

"How's money going to get stuck to my breast?" Natashka's actually groping herself, to make sure there isn't some there already.

"That's what makes it sorcery," Granny Shura yawns. "Now be off with you, girls, because they won't be turning the lights back on until tomorrow, and besides, I need to get some shut-eye."

The friends leave. There's a bright moon in the sky; the snow's glistening; the village sleeps. Even the dogs aren't yapping.

"Shall we go, then?" Lenka's evidently had a fair bit to drink, or she wouldn't be so bold. There's plenty of tattling about her in the village, her being so very keen on folks of the male persuasion. So everyone here knows about that, and who's going to take her to wife? Probably only somebody from Moscow.

Natashka elbows Lyubka. "Let's go," she says. "Maybe it'll work. Or you'll just go on putting one ad after another in the paper, and waiting for what never comes."

And off they go, off down a path that's narrow, but where they can see everything plain as in daylight.

"Wait a minute. I'll fetch a bottle," Lenka says as they draw level with her house. "We'll have a nip or two in the banya."

When they get to Grandpa's banya, the bolt's drawn, so it's not locked. Grandpa must have been bathing and forgotten to lock it back up. They somehow find a candle stub in the darkness and light it, then they drink straight out of the bottle, to work up the nerve.

"Go on, Lyubka. You go first," Natashka says. "It's more important to her. She's a virgin."

"No, I'm first!" Lenka bristles. "Lyubka's young, and I'm ripe and ready and still on the shelf."

"Then it's me." Natashka peels off her sheepskin coat. "I'll be up for my pension soon. You lot wait your turn. We'll do it by age."

Well, so she unbuttons her dress down the front and goes into the banya. It's dark and scary. And all she can think is, why's it so warm? It's not Saturday, so Grandpa won't have been heating it. She stands in the middle of the room and rattles off Granny Shura's charm: "Come, my intended, don't leave me here stranded. Transform into another's hand, show yourself at my command. Deceive me well or love me well..."

Nothing. Nobody grabs her, and there she stands, like a big ninny. But the other girls are piling in from the anteroom, wanting to be next. Lenka's completely undressed, down to her undies, and Lyubka's got nothing on but a t-shirt. And they're all yelling, "Hey, betrothed – one for the road!"

And then the electricity comes back on. The bulb's dim, but you can see everything clear as day. The girls freeze in their tracks. Because on the benches, three guys lie sleeping. They'd come to put a barn up for Grandpa, and he'd let them stay in his banya.

Oh, and what a squealing there was! The guys had the scare of their lives, and the girls bolted away in whatever they'd managed to gather up.

And ever since that day, they've trusted nothing but the cards.

A HELPING HAND

Grandpa Pashka, Pashka Strochkin, was a major. In a tank regiment. He had retired now and come back to the village. But without his tank, of course, he was as bored as he could be, didn't know what to do with himself. He started out by buying a tractor, but what kind of fields do we have around here? Only vegetable plots, and you can't even turn a tractor round in one of those. So he wandered around the village for days on end, wondering how he could make himself useful, what good deed he could do.

The old ladies of our village are a faint-hearted bunch, and there was plenty they needed, what with the potatoes, carrots, and cabbages to plant, and the wood to lay in. Grandpa Pashka decided to take charge of them, since nobody else had them in hand.

He stopped by at Granny Nyura's on his tractor. "It's a fine thing, you digging your potato trenches with a shovel," he says. "Let's plow this up properly. Never despair, I'm here." Uh-huh. So he knocked down Granny Nyura's fence and her woodshed, and churned up the ground so bad you could neither walk nor drive across it. It looked like a tank training ground by the time he was finished.

Then he decided to redo Granny Zina's banya stove, as a sort of surprise. Being hard of hearing, she never heard him proceeding to remodel her banya. But he broke a bunch of bricks while he was dismantling the stove, so Granny Zina had to buy a new cast-iron one, and that ran into some money.

Granny Matryona kept chickens. Grandpa Pashka decided they should be free range, not cooped up, and he let them out. A fox took the one, and a hawk took the other.

The grannies started running away from him. The minute he'd come through the gate, they'd be flapping their hands. "Stay away, for the love of Christ – be off with you," they'd say.

But you can't hold a good tank soldier back. He fixed up one with an antenna, so she could watch television, but she didn't have a television. He started digging a well for another one, but there'd never been any water up on that little hill. It was all down on the flats.

The grannies were in tears, real tears. "Leave us in peace," they'd beg. "What a fuss and bother you cause us, it's horrible. Split us some wood and have done." But what's firewood splitting? It's a week wielding an ax and that's all. Boring.

So Grandpa Pashka decided to take a crack at carpentry. He bought himself a bench and set up a workshop in his little barn. He made benches. But how's a tank-man supposed to know about wood? He installed his benches all over the village, but they had skinny legs, and our grannies are nothing if not hefty, so when they sat down, the benches tipped over and the grannies would be sprawled on the ground, roaring with laughter. Then he made a kennel for Granny Lena's dog, and it was huge as a house. The dog didn't even want to go in there. He was scared he'd get lost.

Meanwhile, Grandpa Pashka was saying how much he liked making things from wood and urging people to write notes on what they needed.

Then winter was on its way. Our grannies sleep on top of their stoves in the winter, to stay warm and not get sick. It's quite a clamber to get up there, but the grannies have been making it work for the lon-　　　　　　gest time. They shuffle a trunk over and stack a stool on top of that, and up they go.

Grandpa Pashka gave that a good look and said, "This'll never do. I'm going to make ladders. I've seen them in pictures, with railings and all. Just what the doctor ordered – evenly spaced rungs, and you're up and down in a snap."

And didn't the grannies just run from him, but he finally caught one. Granny Nyura was built big – as broad as a ship's stern, when you looked at her from behind. She could only go through doors sideways, that's how big she was. And getting up on the sleeping platform took her half a day, with rest breaks. Grandpa Pashka couldn't have been happier. "You'll remember me all your days," he said. "I'm going to make your life so much easier."

He spent a week hanging around Granny Nyura's hut, measuring everything with a tape measure, writing down measurements, and shoving pictures under her nose. Meanwhile, Granny Nyura was crossing herself. "Heck with him, the hobgoblin," she said. "Let him do what he wants, just so long as he doesn't knock my stove down." And she went about her business.

In the meantime, Grandpa Pashka got the ladder done.

He'd made it like they showed in a book, so it would take Granny Nyura's weight, and that's why it came out so heavy, he couldn't lift it by himself. And there you go, he made a deal with some men from the neighboring village. It took three of them to carry the big heavy thing. But they couldn't get it into the hut. They took out a window to squeeze it through, and broke the glass. Granny Nyura was crying, but who was going to listen to her? They got it in, but then it wouldn't fit between the wall and the stove. Grandpa Pashka had got his measurements mixed up somehow.

So they had to take down the room divider, because what wouldn't you do to make things good for Granny Nyura? She came up, looked warily at the ladder, stepped onto the bottom rung, and it was sound. Good. "Well," she thinks. "Now I'll live like a queen in winter!"

When winter came and everyone was snowed in, Pashka Strochkin had up and gone hunting with his friends. Now the grannies were crying their heads off. "Wouldn't you know?" they said. "Just when you need him, he's not here. Who's going to shovel the paths through the snow for us?"

They set about it themselves, got out their shovels and flung the snow every which way, roaring with laughter like young things. But Granny Nyura's such a size, she didn't need a track cleared, she needed a highway. After stomping around a while on her porch, she thought she'd climb up on the stove to warm up. The stove had been stoked; the heat was floating round the hut; there were potatoes in a cast-iron pot on the stove, and some milk, and water boiling in the kettle and rattling the lid.

Granny Nyura took a bit of bread and climbed up. Big rungs, just right for her feet. She was praising Pashka, was tickled pink. Once on her sleeping platform, she made herself comfy, plumped her pillow, then managed to give the ladder an accidental knock with her foot, and it teetered for a moment and toppled over. Pashka had forgotten to attach it.

What a picture it was, with Granny Nyura sitting on top of the stove, chewing on her bread, and weeping bitter tears. And it was snowing like mad outside. The whole night went by, and the next day, and the next. The grannies couldn't clear a way for themselves, so they were stuck at home; they'd all stocked up on wood, and they had water. But they were sitting close to the ground, while Granny Nyura was tucked in under the ceiling. Oh dear. She looked down and her head spun. It was no joke, nearly five feet, as far down as she was tall. Her cat came to join her, and there they sat. She'd probably have to live like that until spring, because there was no way she could get herself down.

The good thing was, the mail lady had started bringing round the pensions. "Where's Granny Nyura?" she asked. They dug her place out and went in – and no Granny. Oh dear. Surely somebody hadn't stolen her away? No, Granny's in tears on the stove, calling, "Dear hearts, get me down!" And that's when they put the trunk back where it belonged and stacked a stool on top of it.

After Grandpa Pashka got home, he went to see Granny Nyura. "Now then," he asked her. "How are you?" And didn't he get an earful! Pashka's not easily scared, though. "So I made a teeny mistake with the ladder height," he said. "And besides, what business do you have climbing up so high? I'll make you a sleeping bench down below. Like a bed it'll be, and we'll put a little stove underneath it. How about that?"

She hurled a cast-iron pot at him, but how's that going to frighten a tankman? He was already busy making mouse traps for Granny Zina, and the other grannies were arguing about whether she'd end up caught in one or if she'd come up lucky for once.

A KNIGHT BRAVE AND BOLD

Lyubka was standing in the yard, dolefully gazing at the pig. It had wrecked its pen and was now out trampling the vegetable garden. "Lyoshka!" she yelled, from force of habit, before stopping short, because, whether called or not, he wouldn't come. Her son had been taken into the army during the spring draft, along with another dozen or so local rubes just like him. The city boys, the ones with money, wormed their way out of it or signed up for college, but the village lads went where they were sent, every last one of them. Still, after the army they might be able to score a job in some city or other, as a security guard if nothing else. There was no work in the village and no pay for whatever work there was. Anyone who stayed got blind drunk or started a sporadic side hustle with the seasonal visitors, mowing their grass in summer and chopping wood or shoveling snow in winter.

Her son, Lyoshka, was good with his hands (if not with his head). He drank (but not too much), could drive a tractor and a car, could take apart a motor and fix a television. Now, after three months without him, Lyubka was starting to think that Lyoshka was simply the perfect son, although only six months earlier she'd been chasing him around the village with an oven fork after finding out that he'd made off with the money she'd been putting aside for her old age.

Lyubka looked down at her feet; yesterday's rain had turned the yard into an impassable mud puddle. She'd asked her son umpteen times to spread sand there but could never quite get through to him. The fence on the street side had rotted way back when and was now splayed out like a fan, so Lyubka had to keep patching it up with wooden slats. But the outside privy was the worst. It too had rotted long ago and collapsed onto the neighbor's property. In winter, you could go in a bucket in the entryway, but that was no good at all in summer, and Lyoshka kept promising to put up a new outhouse, but, as usual, he hadn't done a thing. Everything was falling apart

before their very eyes, and there was no money to make it right, and Lyubka's meager pension melted away within a week after she got it.

Her way had been to deny herself everything, for so long she couldn't even remember when she had last splurged on anything beyond the chemical-pink sausage that even looked raw, pasta that clumped up when you cooked it, and cheap tea that left an aftertaste of dust broom. Whatever she pocketed by selling pork for the November celebrations she put away, being always mindful that in Russia, a rainy day can come out of nowhere.

Lyubka had been born in the USSR. She remembered the collective farm workers not getting the internal passports that allowed them to travel within the country until 1974, when she was in first grade. And in a jiffy, half the village had taken off to the cities.

Life settled down in the late seventies. A hardscrabble life it might have been, but at least they weren't still on the barter system, being issued produce or goods pegged to the number of "workday units" they'd amassed. No, they were now paid in cash.

Lyubka's mother and father broke their backs for the collective farm and for themselves too. They'd gone in with Grandma on three cows, selling the milk and pilfering grain and cattle fodder wherever they could. And Dad siphoned gas from the collective farm's truck. So there was money, but nowhere to spend it. Lyubka remembered her mother and father counting out the crumpled one-ruble notes and deciding what they were going to buy in town. They even bought her older brother a motorcycle with a sidecar, which the whole family, guffawing and singing, rode out into the fields to mow hay or to the forest to pick berries. Then her brother had died in Afghanistan, and Lyubka remembered her mother crying out and banging her head against the stove's whitewashed side, and her father sitting in silence, tapping his knife point on the table.

After Lyubka's brother died, her mother took to her bed, the illnesses coming one after the other. Her father started off by going into town with his ailing wife, but then gave up and just let it be. Already a drinking man, he now hit the bottle in good earnest, beating on Lyubka and her mother both, and one time, after getting hammered at the regional center, he tumbled out of the bed of a big old truck and fell to his death.

Like the other girls in her class, Lyubka had dreamed of going to study in town, but instead she stayed in the village, because there was no one to care for her sick mother, and besides, she couldn't just let the house go like that. She was hired by the collective farm's bookkeeping office. It was a cushy job that paid on time, and she and the young chairman hit it off, and he threw her an extra ruble or two, for giving him some good loving off the clock.

He couldn't marry her, being married already, and he was scared stiff of being called on the carpet by the Party. Lyubka gave birth to a daughter and kept waiting for the chairman to claim the child as his, but he up and left, and then, all of a sudden, perestroika began, and nothing made sense anymore, but in the village there was a whiff of something new and dangerous that didn't yet have a name. Lyubka carried on working for the new management, sent her daughter to the collective farm's kindergarten, and thought and thought of ways to leave that dump of a village behind and head off to start a new life.

She'd never been to a big city, like Moscow. She'd never even been farther than the district center, where all of twenty thousand people lived. And she fancied the world out there to be like in a Bollywood movie – gold galore, fountains, marble, and lovely girls in colorful dresses, all singing and dancing. But back home in Russia, things were bubbling over. The talkative one with the red splotch on his head made way for a gray-haired good-looker, also a talker, and everybody told Lyubka that happiness lay ahead but for the time being, she should hold on. And this was nothing new to Lyubka, so she held on and waited for a better life, like the rest of the country.

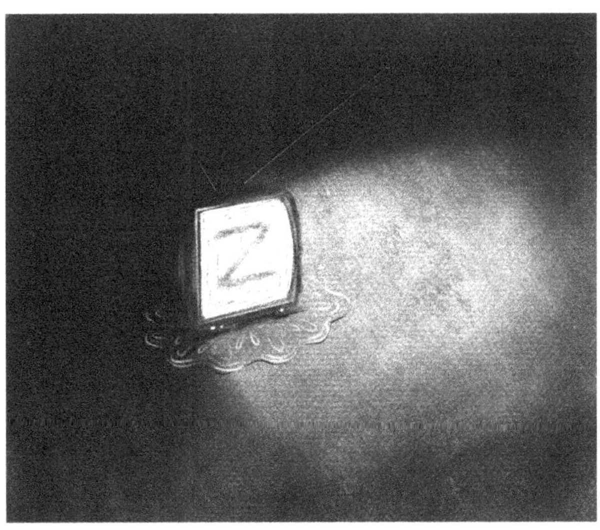

The money disappeared. Groceries got expensive in a hurry, and then they disappeared too, and for long enough that the only thing you could count on was yourself. At which point, the earth that feeds us all came to the rescue. The cow gave milk, and that made sour cream, cottage cheese, butter, and thick, tangy buttermilk. The hens laid eggs. The vegetable garden gave everything anyone could need, from potatoes to cucumbers. The forest gave berries and mushrooms. Lyubka even learned to make jam without sugar and to produce a home brew from grain and stolen molasses.

In 2000, a new guy took over at the top, and Lyubka liked him. He was young, all smiles, so modest. He dressed simply, whether on a plane flight or at a church service, and he spoke persuasively, and he even had that funny line about "capping 'em in the lavatory." And he too promised a better life.

Lyubka, who had been waiting for that better life since the day she was born, had no problems holding on, and she gave birth to Lyoshka, her Aleksei, fathered by a seasonal visitor who had come to stay with his neighbors from town and get some fishing in. After Lyubka called him from the post office to tell him he had a son, he didn't pick up her calls any more and never came back to the village, but Lyubka didn't take that amiss. Her daughter was married and had left by then, and now Lyoshka was there, to warm his mother's heart.

Thinking about her son, Lyubka came so unglued that she said to hell with the pig and went back into the house, to the living quarters that had been Lyoshka's before the army. Her face pressed into the pillow that still smelled of him, Lyubka dozed off and dreamed that her son was riding in a tank, going to fight the Nazis. The Nazis were in black uniforms with silver trim, while Lyoshka was dressed like a Russian knight of yore, brave and bold, wearing chain mail and a helmet. On he rode, looking into the distance, a hand shading his eyes, and the frightened Nazis scattered. In her dream, Lyubka was as proud of her son as a mother could be and wept with happiness, and on waking, she thought, "When Lyoshka passes away, they'll pick a street in the village and name it after him."

AVDOTYA AND THE DISTRICT MEDIC

The little hospital on the outskirts of the village is shrouded by a young pine wood as if to keep it from the prying eyes of healthy folks. But it's been a long time since this place housed the ailing or resounded with the dull moans and sudden shrieks of some poor soul having his sore tooth yanked out by a merciless medic with a pair of iron forceps.

Now the door, painted a playful green, is locked up tight with a big, clunky padlock that's hanging upside-down, and a gentle breeze is ruffling the sheet of notebook paper that gives the times when the district medic will be by to see patients. The ink on the paper has smeared; the tack holding it to the door has rusted.

With their backs to the sun-warmed clinic wall, the gals sit, their Chinese padded jackets unbuttoned, showing the colorful sweaters knitted from sheep's wool that they wear underneath. The benches lost their legs a long while ago, but they've been pushed up against an earth mound to keep them upright. There's not a lick of space on the benches, by reason of the gals being so broad in the beam. Plus, they're bookended by old geezers, two of them. One, scrawny and hoary-headed, is smoking, and the other, hefty and short-winded, is blowing his nose into a woman's kerchief and breathing heavy.

And as they wait, they do their share of grumbling.

"Oh girls," moans the one in the middle with a nose like a duck bill, Avdotya's her name. "Why'm I sitting and sitting here, when the cow's to be milked, the sheep ain't been watered, the piglet ain't been slopped, the chickens've plowed up the vegetable patch like a dashed tractor, and what're we waiting for?"

"Because he's got things to do before he gets to us," replies Nikitichna, round as a ball of butter. "Getting here, I was aching all over, and that one there, the doc – he's probably home having tea. Vas! Hey, Vas!" She's talking to the scrawny geezer in the fur hat. "Have a look, will you, and see what time it says."

Vasily stands up reluctantly, dragging his left foot. He limps to the porch, takes his spectacles out of a plastic case, and peers at the sheet of paper.

"It don't say nothing about no clinic hours," he croaks. "It's about vaccinations for the cows."

The gals break into merry laughter, elbowing each other.

"There you go! We're cows, that we are. All our lives long we're getting milked, having our tails tugged, and there's no good to be had from us."

"I only wish we got fertilizer from you too." That's the other geezer, Pyotr Nikanorych, who held every high-level job there was on the collective farm, from agronomist to engineer, and therefore knows his stuff and is skeptical about life in general. "What is a cow?" he continues, raising a finger to the sky. "A dumb beast. Pay that some mind, now, and given that you're cattle, don't be bothering the health service for no good reason."

The gals turn their backs on him as one, which nearly makes the bench topple over. Avdotya, a beauty in her younger days, pouts her lips and straightens her gaudy kerchief with its shiny metallic threads. Then she swivels around and calls out to a gal with plump cheeks and a veiny nose.

"Parasha! Hey, Parasha!" she says. "Did you get something to take away the rheumatiz in your joints?"

"That I did, like all the others," Parasha replies, her chin propped on a gnarled walking stick. "Like my mama and my grandma. And my great…"

"Hold up, chatterbox. Stop your jibber-jabber and tell what you did about it."

"With chicken droppings," the thoroughly offended Parasha responds. "Only not fresh droppings, they'll scorch. The aged stuff's good, though. If it's been aging the whole winter, now that's the ticket. You pull a bunch of nettles, young so they'll sting something awful, pound them with the droppings, and put it all on a cloth. You bind up the sore spot and then more droppings and then more nettles. Then wrap it well. Oh, it burns all right, girls! You'll cuss up a storm – a thunderstorm, even!"

Already Avdotya's not convinced. "Don't the skin come off?" she asks. "How long'll it be before the bones get eaten away?"

"So smear on some pounded pig lard. Beaver fat's good, yup … And put an ordinary pair of stockings round it. Instead of a compress."

"Really?" Avdotya unbuttons her sweater and kneads her chest. "It's so hot nowadays ... everything's burning up... Down to brass tacks, though – does it help?"

Parasha rubs her knees. "Damned if I know. I go for a jab too. Something helps, but I dunno which."

Then scrawny Vasya butts in. "Well now, ladies, what would you do for a cough? I've been hacking my lungs out ever since the war."

"I've got something for you, Vasily Kuzmich." That's the other Parasha getting in on the act. As a former store manager, she's respected in the village and is always up on everything. "You'll need a sack."

"And what's that for? To haul me off to the graveyard?" Vasya asks huffily.

"Not a bit of it. You'll need a potato sack, like. Clean, though, laundered proper. And in Maytime, when birch sap runs and the beetles're flying, pull off some birch leaves and dry them."

The gals remember then. "That's just it!" they say. "It's coming back to me now." "Just it!" "Even in hospitals they treated consumptives that way, indeed they did."

"Stuff the sack full of leaves and tie it round your throat."

"Won't I suffocate?"

"I've yet to hear of any such thing. Take to your bed, sweat it out, and it's good to rub the soles of your feet with lard. Uh-huh. Or with beaver fat."

"And what about the innards?' Vasily Kuzmich's lips are moving, as if he's taking a drink. "Next thing we know, you'll be recommending turpentine or the like!"

"For that you'll want swamp-root," Pyotr Nikanorych pipes up, spitting into the goutweed that has just started sprouting by the bench. "All your turpentine does is stink up the place. You need to dig up some devyasil root." He pronounces it "devil seal." "It looks like a beet on top, but break it and it's pure chalk inside. Pound it up and drink it in fortified wine. And what you can't get down, rub it in where it hurts."

"If you men would do anything except drink yourselves blotto, you wouldn't need no doctoring," the gals chorus. "Government's got no business doctoring you at all. A good thrashing with nettles'd put you right back on your feet."

Avdotya rifles around in her wheeled tote for a copy of *Arguments and Facts*, smooths it out on her knees, adjusts her spectacles, and starts reading out loud.

She begins with the "Health" section. The gals listen, motionless. But when the newspaper's been read, off they go again.

"The lumbago needs to be beat out of you. There was this old gal, way out in Ostov, and she could beat with the best. Put a banya switch on the sore place and lay into it with the butt of an axe. No more bad back then."

"And one time this lady medic came and said to mix up some of the old-style flu powder, add kerosene and vinegar, and then…"

"You're pulling our legs! Kerosene! You'll go up in flames."

"What's needed is to collect the cracked stones out of the banya stove, and put it on the small of the back…"

Then an off-road vehicle pulls up and a tired-looking, dusty district medic jumps out of the passenger seat, carrying a gray metal case. He smokes a cigarette on the porch, neatly flicks the butt into a red-painted bucket, and proceeds to lay down the law.

"In the order you signed up, girls! We aren't here all day! Step lively, grannies!"

An hour later, all is quiet. The gals are standing in a circle, waiting for the bus.

"What did he prescribe, then?" The oldster scratches under his cap. "Animal dung or chicken droppings?"

Avdotya sounds it out. "It's an-al-gee-sick," she says. "And some sort of oily stuff, can't say off the top of my head. I'll be going to the healer woman, and I can buy my own an-al-gee-sick, don't need no doc for that. A waste of time is all it was…"

SOCKS

Grandpa Vitka Samokhin always trusted the television. There was no one to talk to in the village, but in the television there lived pleasant, respectful – though sometimes high-strung – people he could chat with. Vitka also kept up to date on the map that showed how the military operation was going, though the flags on it never had to be rearranged. The front line was at a standstill.

He would peer through the window at the snow lying on the house roofs and covering the barns and even the post office, and feel blue. He imagined the front from the tales told by his pa, Pyotr Samokhin, who had been caught up in the dreadful bloodbath at Velikie Luki in the winter of 1942. The young Vitka also remembered Dad complaining to his old lady, not about being afraid to die, but about his feet being frozen all the time. Now Vitka wondered to himself how that could be. Tanks, planes, and his dad shivering with cold in his felt boots.

Vitka thought a while longer and watched some more television, listened to that one commentator who got worked up so easily and always scared him with his cussing and his arm-waving, and decided that the front needed help. The very next morning, trampling the snow under his old felt boots in their new, glossy, black overshoes, he ran around the village, trying to prod the grannies into showing what they were made of. They weren't too eager to be prodded, all being as old as could be, but there was no getting away from him.

"Get this, you old dimwit" Vitka was pounding on Granny Nyura's table. "Their feet are freezing out there. It's winter, winter everywhere. But you, you pair of old galoshes, you don't give a rap."

He frightened Granny Liza so much that she dead-bolted her door from the inside and listened to him through the keyhole.

"Liza, you tightwad!" Vitka howled, hopping around the porch like a hare. "You've got thousands of knit socks. Hand them over: the Motherland needs them."

Worn out by Vitka's yelling, Granny Liza cleared her throat. "To heck with you, you bald-headed devil," she said. "They're new. What if I get married? They'll be my dowry. I'm not giving them to you! Go find some wool, and I'll knit it up, but don't you touch what's mine."

Granny Ulyana cried her eyes out when she heard Vitka's tale, because she didn't watch television. She had nothing like that at home except the district newspaper that came to her mailbox.

"I'll knit some socks, Vitka," she said, wiping her tears. "Why wouldn't I? You think I don't understand? But where is that country – the one where our lads have gone?"

Grandpa Vitka couldn't really explain to the old girl where Ukraine was, but managed to persuade her that it was way up in the frigid North.

Once armed with the agreement of all the available old ladies, Vitka went on a search for wool. They hadn't kept sheep in the village for the longest time; the wool-carding shop had been shut down in 2004; the old ladies had sold their drop spindles to the summer visitors; and the most ancient board distaff with its horizontal base had been carted off to the local history museum. Vitka was so put out that he decided to get the grannies to give up the goods whether they wanted to or not, like in the good old Soviet times.

"Come on, girls," he shouted in the store when they were buying stale loaves and granulated sugar. "Hand over all your knitwear. We'll unravel it. We'll wind it into skeins. And we'll knit it up."

The old girls weren't born yesterday. They didn't care to give up their new goat-wool scarves or their patterned woolen sweaters. On top of that, Granny Liza, a handicrafter in her younger days, had worked her knit tops with colorful embroidered flowers, roosters, and shining suns.

"How," she wanted to know, "am I going to hand these lovely things over to you? For socks, so the heels can be worn into holes? Nope, I'm not handing them over just to make socks! But I can knit a soldier's sweater with a turtleneck and an embroidered portrait of a general – you want that?"

An exasperated Vitka brushed her off. "You're a nitwit," he said, "If everyone in the company gets one, then yes. But what if there's just the one, and the general gets it? The others'll all be green with envy. Still, you can embroider letters, the permitted letters – nobody says you can't."

Granny Nyura, the one Vitka pestered the most, brought a bundle of her grandfather's old things, and, sitting at Vitka's table, unraveled each one, filling the air with dust and rattling on about life as it used to be, which was a whole lot better than now, because people kept sheep back then and Nyura – well, Nyura was young.

Granny Ulyana suddenly remembered that a good eight years ago she'd hung skeins of bleached wool to dry in the attic and forgotten about them. The attic door was forced open, but the skeins had been eaten by bugs and weren't good for much at all.

Vitka's energy reached all the way to the district center, where his distant relatives lived, and they sent him a sackful of colored yarn. Now it was all but a done deal: Vitka just had to pass the wool out to the grannies and wait while they knitted the socks.

The grannies acted up, wanted nothing to do with the skeins from town, because that wasn't real wool, they said. It was squeaky and gave every sign of not having been sheared from a sheep at all. Vitka talked them into it, though, and settled down to wait. And, so the time would go faster, he started a batch of moonshine. "Socks are all well and good," he reasoned to himself, "but vodka warms like nothing else."

The first run he drank himself – because you can't send an untested product as a gift – then went wandering around the village, singing the wartime song about Katyusha. He had to know just how strong the moonshine needed to be before it would help a man survive the bitter cold.

"It's an experiment," he told the grannies. "I'm testing it on myself."

The roofs started dripping; March had come; and the grannies brought Vitka a sack full of socks. Funny-looking they were, all different-colored stripes, and they squeaked like the snow.

"Lovely" Vitka said, clearly dubious about his neighbors' hard work. Then, slinging the sack across his back and picking up his canisters of moonshine, he took the bus to town. And there they laughed at him. The distribution of moonshine was forbidden, and the socks turned out to be worse than useless because summer was coming and besides, who fights in felt boots these days?

Upset, Vitka went straight to the market, sold his moonshine, and bought a sheep. She bleated and didn't want to go anywhere by bus, but Vitka, hinting broadly that even a sheep could come to a bad end, finally crammed her on board and made a happy journey home, listening to the sheep bleating and thinking about how she would have lambs and the village would be teeming with sheep, which meant that there'd be socks aplenty, once there was something to knit them from.

NIKOLAYEV AND LYUSKA

Nikolayev hated the cat, wet socks, and his mother-in-law. The socks would get wet because his boots had holes; the mother-in-law would nag him for having done away with her daughter's happiness; and the cat just peed in his cap if he dozed off on the floor. Taking on his mother-in-law was pointless. That sprightly old gal could easily dodge an oven fork brandished in her direction, she checked the stools to make sure a leg hadn't been sawn through, and she never drank tea that Nikolayev had brewed.

The sock thing was worse.

His mother-in-law knitted the socks, so he had to humiliate himself by sneaking them from her stash. She counted them and made notches on the windowsill for any that were stolen. When the tally topped a half-dozen pairs, she would start whining for money or promising to call in the local constable. The windowsill was slashed and scored like a lace doily.

The cat's name was Lyuska. Her mother, decrepit old Muska, had kept on having litter after litter until she finally ran out of steam, gave birth to a runt, and quietly died. The wife and mother-in-law promptly lost their minds. They fed the kitten from an eyedropper, holding their breath. That little thing reminded them something awful of their beloved Muska.

From that point on, the cat was spoiled rotten and had no respect for Nikolayev as a man and the head of the family. After a day of torment on his bumpy, rackety tractor, all he wanted was a drink and a good sleep, but the cat had her own opinion on that. A couple of times she had blithely swatted his half-pint of vodka off the table, which got her flung out the ventilation window. And there it was: they were at war.

Lyuska would lie in wait until Nikolayev sat down to supper and, purring quietly, would sneak up from behind, sweeping the floor with her tail, and latch onto his calf, chomping down on it with her sharp teeth. Then off she scampered, to hide beneath

the floorboards. Nikolayev would go after her, and never mind if his mother-in-law and wife tried to get in his way. After a while, he would give up in disgust and go to get some shut-eye on the stove, under his granddad's cozy homespun coat, which Lyuska had managed to soak in between times. She gnawed Nikolayev's leather boots, which let even more water in, and raked his felt boots with her claws.

Fresh from the banya on his days off, Nikolayev would sit at the table in his knee-length sateen undershorts and striped t-shirt, his eyes slitted with happiness, chugging beer from an enameled milk can and snacking on onion and herring. Lyuska, neatly netted beforehand, would be howling balefully in the storage chest. And that's how they lived, until Nikolayev broke his leg. He flat out refused to check himself in at the clinic, having decided that he'd rather put up with his mother-in-law than a dozen ward-mates.

That was when Lyuska changed. Too weak to lift a finger, Nikolayev lay in a listless rage, feeling the cat eyeing him from the stove. Eventually she plucked up courage and started coming down, even lying on the little mat by the bed. Then she'd be jumping onto the beat-up sofa. Once, when the mother-in-law was making a din with her pots and buckets, Lyuska pricked up her ears and started gently sharpening her claws on Nikolayev's plaster cast.

Sick and tired of being laid up, Nikolayev actually took to sharing his troubles with Lyuska and feeding her bits of the cheese that his mother-in-law made. Before the week was out, he couldn't go an hour without worrying whenever Lyuska launched her bulky self through the ventilation window. She had her litter at night, waking Nikolayev with a strange snuffling and rustling in the sheets.

He didn't sleep a wink, for fear of moving his leg in its plaster cast. It was not until morning that he called out – softly, feebly – "Mother dear, where're you at? I've got kittens here."

"Oh, botheration!" his mother-in-law wailed. "And you with a gimpy leg, so who'll do the drowning?"

"I'll kill *you*," Nikolayev said crisply, reaching for his crutches.

He let all six of them be.

SISTERS IN SORROW

On Saturdays, Polina fires up the banya, washes down her hut, and beats the rugs. For her, this is party time. Her husband took off long ago, but Polina wasn't too broken up about that: he never brought in much money, he drank, was quick with his fists, so what fun was he? Polina has wangled herself a pension from her years working for the timber company, her older son tosses a bit of cash her way now and again (pretty good to his mother, he is), so she's actually living the good life. She has it all, and the village isn't even a village anymore. It's a proper town.

She has a washing machine, and a vacuum cleaner, and a new television that takes up a whole wall. The television is Polina's pride and joy. The colors are turned way up, painfully bright – so lovely, just like at the movies, Polina would sigh. The only pity is that the television being on the wall means you can't put a doily on top.

The television is her only confidant, her only friend and advisor. Recently, mind you, it's been all politics, with the men yelling and arguing and the women shrieking and saying scary things. But Polina has learned to get along with them. "Come on, now," she'd say. "Shush, or I'll turn you off!" She argues with them, or perhaps she agrees. The noisiest of the lot, the one with a fat, meaty face, makes good points, gets it right every time. When Polina listens to him, she always thinks of the peddler from the district center who used to sell all sorts of Chinese-made junk door-to-door, and the way he talked, you'd stand there and listen and always end up buying something.

Polina couldn't have been happier. "It's good now," she thinks, "because how many newspapers would you have to wade through before, and they all wrote the same thing, dull as could be. And now look! It doesn't bother him a bit to say bad words, and that tells you he's not lying. But how come he doesn't get an earful from his bosses?"

Polina wipes the television with a cloth and picks up her bag. She's heading for the banya when, wouldn't you know it, the telephone starts chirping. On the screen,

there's a color photo of Marina, her younger sister, identified as "Birdbrain." Polina purses her lips, reluctantly sets her bag on the floor, and picks up the phone.

"Hello, is that you, Marina?"

"Like you can't see," the caller snipes back, cranky as ever. "I bet you have me in your contacts as 'Ninny,' like I don't know any better."

The sisters have been feuding since they were little. Polina, always the boss, needled Marina on purpose, and the younger girl whined and cried and complained to Mom and Dad. Their father made short work of it, smacking them both on the back of the head just in case. He didn't feel bad for his girls. The one thing he did feel bad about was that his wife hadn't given him any boys.

The two of them went to the eight-grade village school and brought home middling grades, except that Polina was more perky and did well in the Komsomol. People thought she'd end up in the district center or maybe even in Moscow. But she never did. Instead, she rushed into marriage and got herself a job as a rate clerk at the timber company.

"Look, girls," she'd say. "I have so much of everything – sacks of money, a husband, a home, and a car, and there you are, carping and grousing and envying me."

And the whole village surely did envy her, for having so much happiness all to herself.

In the nineties, a lumber company was started up in the village, a joint venture with people from Germany. The Germans came, yammering away in their outlandish language, though to this day the folks in the village can't bear to hear German spoken. Still, they bit their tongues, because money's money.

There was, truth be told, no one to interpret, until somebody remembered Marina. She'd studied German and was able enough. Peter, an engineer, fell in love with her straight off and stuck to her like glue. The whole village poked fun. "Lookit, here comes Marina's Fritz," they'd say, and she'd bristle but shrug it off. "It's Peter," she'd tell them. "Is that so hard to remember? Pyotr, just plain Pyotr, to you."

Once the place was up and running, her German went home. He sent letter after letter and pretty cards at Christmas, with Santa Claus and sleighs pulled by reindeer. He sent those letters, but he never came himself. Marina got tired of waiting and decided to put in an application to move to town and go to a technical college, because now she couldn't even walk through the village in peace, not with all the taunting.

So off she went to the bus stop with her suitcase. And on that very bus was Peter, coming from town. For her.

Her sister Polina told her what a ninny she was, how she must be out of her mind to marry a German. "He killed our granddad," she said, "and he killed half the village, and you're a traitor, that's what you are."

Marina shrugged that ancient history off and left. Ever since then, she'd been living far away, in the city of Hanover, and driving her older sister distracted. She would send huge packages crammed with beautiful things, such good quality too, and Polina couldn't figure out which of the two of them was living better. Hadn't Polina's people won?

So now she's talking through gritted teeth into the phone.

"A lot you know. I've got your photo here, from the year before last, and it says 'Marina.' Do you remember when we went to Grandma's to help bring in the hay?"

Marina softens and goes on and on, saying how much she misses them and how good it would be to see her nephew, the older one, and asking how the younger one's doing and if it's true that he's been drafted.

"He's been drafted," Polina says gruffly. "So what? Everyone's been drafted. We're all waiting for you Germans to attack us. You and your NATO."

While Marina's telling her that no one's about to attack anyone, Polina's remembering what the fat-face on TV has been saying, and rattles it off pretty much word for word. "We'll take Berlin and that Vienna of yours," she says, "and then we'll show you what's what." Her younger sister's sniffling on the other end of the line, but Polina, her brain all aflame with the sound bites she's learned by rote, goes on scolding her for living with the enemy instead of doing the right thing and coming home to her Motherland.

"Have they drafted Viktor, though?" Marina brings it up out of the blue. "He's the right age, and he's had that special training."

"They'll be drafting him soon," Polina says with pride. "And I'll sign up too, if it comes to that."

"If you want, I can hide him away here, 'cos he's got a passport for travel abroad," Marina jabbers. "He's my nephew. I feel so bad for him, I can't do this anymore."

Polina cuts her short. "We don't need that, but you and your... Pyotr can come here if you want. For the winter. Because they told us on the television that you've got no gas for heat, no water, no light, no way to wash, and it's cold. And we've got three winters' worth of firewood, there's water in the well, and they hardly ever turn the lights off. Come, sister." Suddenly Polina's sniffling too. "Come. We'll make it through the winter somehow – the more, the merrier..."

The banya cooled off a long while ago, but Polina is still sitting on the wobbly stool her father made, complaining to her sister in faraway Germany that there's no money, and the gas has gone up, and they're going to draft Viktor and she'll be alone, all alone. And on the other end, in the neon-flooded city of Hanover, on the second floor of a building on Bremer Damm, Marina sits in a comfy armchair, and the Christmas tree, decorated with silver bells, winks at her, through tears.

CUCUMBERS

Lyusya Kamyshova, known to all as Lyuska-Cuke, sowed her cucumbers all out of season that year. Not like any normal person – on the fifth of June, the feast day of St. Leonty of the Cucumbers – oh no! In March, if you please.

"What a life," Lyusya said to herself, as she and her friends were downing cheap wine in the empty clubhouse. "What a life. But if the cucumbers freeze all to hell, I'll be free for the whole year, have time to work out what makes me happy."

The thing is that Lyusya was famous village-wide as Yamtsovo's most successful cucumber farmer. Cucumbers were birthed all over the village but, either because the Yamtsovites were too greedy or because the weather could be less than cooperative, they always came out as enormous as hot air balloons or as crooked as Grandpa Matvey's fingers, or shriveled, or shaped like a light bulb or a mini-cantaloupe. Only Lyusya's were high grade and easy to recognize by variety – some cornichons for pickling, some salad cucumbers to be sliced just so, some neither massive nor too small but sweet enough to feed to little kids, some with black spines, prickly, for the cold brining known as monastery style. And the yellow, seedy, huge, depressed-looking ones Lyusya picked early, so that no one would walk off with them, horning in on her priceless stash of cucumber seeds.

All summer the rumpus went on around the hothouses, the open beds, the special planters raised high off the ground from which twined the "Indian lianas" – to wit, our own, dear, darling Russian cucumbers.

Lyusya never left off fussing over her cucumbers, not even for a day. She loosened the soil, pulled up the pesky weeds, and liberally dispensed a reddish-brown mash that stank so bad even the moles would crawl, sneezing, from their burrows. She'd have friendly talks with the cucumbers, scold them, chivvy them along, take them to task, sing to them (insisting that their favorite songs were "Chamomiles Have Hidden, Buttercups Have Withered" and "The White Steamship"). Everywhere labels

were driven into the soil – home-made plant labels, a stick split at the top that held a piece cut from a beer can. They could be written on with a felt-tip marker and later wiped clean, to be used again next year.

And was there any variety she didn't grow? There were Vyaznik cucumbers, and Nezhin cucumbers, needless to say, and Cornichon de Paris, and Rodnichok, and April, and Zozulya... Each variety was valuable in its own way, either because of where they grew best, in a greenhouse or an open bed under the sun, or because of their yield, or because of their time to harvest. In the warm June nights, the skinny little cucumber stems would pop up, their yellow caps soon turning into tasty little cucumbers, either hairy or prickly.

"Cucumber, cucumber – in the belly you don't slumber," Lyusya would say over and over, as she carefully placed the cucumbers into a basket lined with straw. "Dandies chew candies, but it's cucumbers for the likes of us." "Oh, a man to remember, with a nose like a cucumber!" she'd holler as she weeded the rows. And "Briny, briny cucumber, greedy little hog; no one'll ever eat you if you tumble off that log" and "Out came the drunkards to pick over the cucumbers." And the rest of it was not fit for polite company, but as salty as it needed to be.

The seasonal visitors came to Lyusya along with the locals, to sort through her tender, subtly fragrant wares, not to mention the fresh, cucumber-flavored borage that perfumes salads in such a special way. Lyusya sold seasonings too, but shiftily and a little dishonestly, and to all tricky questions on the lines of "How much garlic do you put in, Lyusya?" she would reply, scratching her heel on a fence post, "Much as I can spare."

"And how much would that be?" the pushy seasonal visitor, used to measuring everything in ounces, would persist.

"Depends," Lyusya would reply, and vanish behind the fence.

Lyusya made especially good money with her lightly brined, finger-sized cucumbers and the huge ones best fit for plus-sized mouths. She sold them in "batches," avoiding high-flown words like "assortment." She put them into barrels that had first been scalded with a mixture of vinegar and water poured over hot bricks, then she added herbs in addition to the usual garlic, dill, mint, blackcurrant leaves, horseradish leaves, and cherry leaves. Oak leaves made it tart and strong, nettles added a searing delicacy, and the salt always had to be the coarse-grained kind from Iletsk, which brined the cucumbers all the way down to the seeds.

Resistance was pointless. When the men rolled the barrels out to start the selling, the aroma would seep out, taking material form, and creep into everyone's nostrils, awakening an appetite for whatever that person loved the most. The drinkers ran off after a bottle, the womenfolk flung themselves into the boiling of jacket potatoes, the youngsters went to catch them some perch, and those women who were in the family way ate their cucumbers right next to the barrel, not in the least ashamed to be shedding tears of joy.

For the winter, Lyusya cold-brined some cucumbers monastery style, in frigid water with chunks of ice, and put the tubs in the old well, where they stayed until the November celebrations, and some until spring.

But that March, after deciding to get her personal life on track, Lyusya made some paper funnels, mixed soil in them, spat on the seeds she'd chosen, and buried it all in the greenhouse.

"Heck with you," she said. "I can't take it anymore, you green nuisances! We've made a deal: I'll do my civic duty by planting you, you'll freeze, and I'll live in peace."

But the cucumbers knew what was what. They sat quiet through March, then suddenly, in April, got an attitude and sprouted. April came in hot, and already in June, Lyusya was selling the first, crunchy cucumbers in their yellow flower-hats.

"Such is my dismal fate," Lyusya brooded. "It's like the cucumbers take the place for me of a Mommy and a Daddy and a dog named Laddie. There'll be no happiness for me, and I'll never live to have a husband, and a maiden I shall die," she lamented, wiping away the bitter, yet also salty, tears.

But you can't trick fate. The fame of Lyusya's cucumbers reached Moscow, and a whole movie was made about the renowned Lyuska-Cuke and posted on YouTube, and Lyusya had a visit from the famous, the world-famous Rajan Thakur, an Indian whose nickname was Kheera, which is Hindi for… yes, for cucumber. He wanted to talk about best practices.

At first they almost came to blows over who was best at pickling cucumbers, but Rajan fell so deeply in love with Lyusya that he let her be right. They married, Lyusya and Rajan, and lived a long and happy life together, because the folks in India are every bit as keen on cucumbers as the folks in Yamtsovo are, for all that the climate in Uttarakhand is kinder to those much-loved vines.

VALYA AND TOLYA IN FALL

Valya and Tolya Konoplyannikov had divorced two years back after a whole forty-two years of marriage, sent running in different directions by a mutual hostility that had gnawed into their very innards. A village divorce is a tiresome, no-win business. If you're in Moscow, you can move from Beskudnikovo to Novo-Gireyevo and disappear into thin air. But in the village? No dice. You're going to bump into each other at the cooperative store, the post office, or the clinic, and there you'll be, nose to nose, with nowhere to run this time.

And then there's the marital home. How can you possibly split that up? Where do you put the two parts? If someone sneezes at one end of a small village like this, you see, somebody else catches a cold at the other. The Konoplyannikovs divided things up and divided some more, and when all was said and done, Granny Valya stayed in the Konoplyannikov abode, and Grandpa Tolya took himself off to an abandoned hut behind the old state farm's stables. And so, after sharing out the barns, the woodsheds, the cowshed, the bathhouse, the cow, the sheep, the piglet, the chickens, and Tolya's deaf old grandma, they made a fresh start at opposite ends of the village.

Valya's retirement came before Tolya's, and she started living like a princess, spreading store-bought butter on her bread, skipping the potato planting, and going to the dances at the club. But Tolya, now free of the spouse who had once been the love of his life, began pining for her warm back, her thick cabbage soup simmering away in the stove, the funny, gaudy socks she knitted so skillfully on five needles (always forgetting to bind off the heel end properly), and her tuneful snoring that sent him to sleep better than the television. And he hit the bottle. He drank for a week, then gave a thought to his deaf grandma, pined even more than before, and started building a new life, one inspired by the old state farm. "Forward" had been its name, so forward he went. And then cabbage soup came back into the picture, and woolen socks too, because his grandma, deaf as she was, could still wield a set of knitting

needles. He built a new bathhouse, cemented a great big kettle into the stove to supply his hot water, bound together leafy branches to make a winter stash of bathhouse switches, and started waiting for fall to arrive and offer him an escape from the sorrows of his past life.

In fall, everyone in Kolpakovo – old and young alike – quit caring about their daily bread and raced off into the forest, because it was the start of mushroom season. They toted the mushrooms in tightly lidded birchbark buckets, in baskets, in backpacks, or transported them in wheelbarrows, in car trunks, even in tractor carts. So bountiful was the area around Kolpakovo that prominent mycologists would actually publish articles on "the Kolpakovo phenomenon" in scientific journals. Mushrooms sprouted up far and wide. In gloomy stands of spruce, and in patches of birch, and in bashful aspen groves, and in pine thickets free of undergrowth, there were mushrooms everywhere. Some went so far as to grow right under people's windows, along pathways, behind the bathhouse, even by the cooperative store, where a bench had been set firmly into the ground, which was littered with cigarette butts – even here, for better or worse, there'd be death caps poking through.

The folks in Kolpakovo would start by pouncing on every mushroom, but come September they cooled off and started picking only the sturdy little boletuses with their chocolatey-looking caps and the Caesar's mushrooms, for brining. The little boys lobbed russulas at each other and gathered the itty bitty caps of birch boletes, kicking their swollen stems all over the place.

The Konoplyannikovs, no longer husband and wife, started mushrooming solo. Granny Valya would leave her hut on the first side street that meandered leftward from the highway, while Grandpa Tolya would trudge off from the other end of the village. But all roads, as the saying goes, lead to Rome, and they would always be making their way into the forest at the same time. Because there was only one way in. It was where the river that flowed around the mushroom-rich places went all meek and mild, narrowing to a stream and obligingly letting folk stride right over it. Granny Valya, wearing sweatpants and a scarlet checked shirt cinched with a military belt and carrying a birchbark bucket set in her backpack, bore left from the fork in the path, and Grandpa Tolya, wearing identical pants and an identical shirt cinched with an absolutely identical belt, bore right. Tolya, mind you, had ditched the backpack in favor of a birchbark basket that he'd woven himself. And had a lid.

The meeting at the way into the forest caused the former Konoplyannikov couple considerable annoyance mixed with a competitive envy. What if the other one picks more? Makes a better job of it? What if one of them gets ahold of the tiny, robust little boletuses, the sort that are just begging to be canned in brine, and you end up with nothing but flabby old aspen mushrooms and rough-stemmed boletes with spores already spilling from their slack mouths onto the withered grass?

Back in the day, the Konoplyannikovs would roam through the places where mushrooms grew, hallooing and calling to each other, the words winging their way over the spruce saplings: "You got anything, Valya?" "Not a thing here, Tolya. How about you?" Valya – young then, a chubby cheeked cutie – would give a whispered gasp when she discovered a whole clutch of prized white mushrooms under the low-hanging spruce boughs, and Tolya would "oooh" and "aaah" when he happened on a family of Caesar's mushrooms nestled comfortably among the roots of a pine. And then, calling back and forth loudly enough to drown out and fluster the forest's bird population, they would hurry toward each other, perch on a fallen tree, and upend their baskets to tip out their haul.

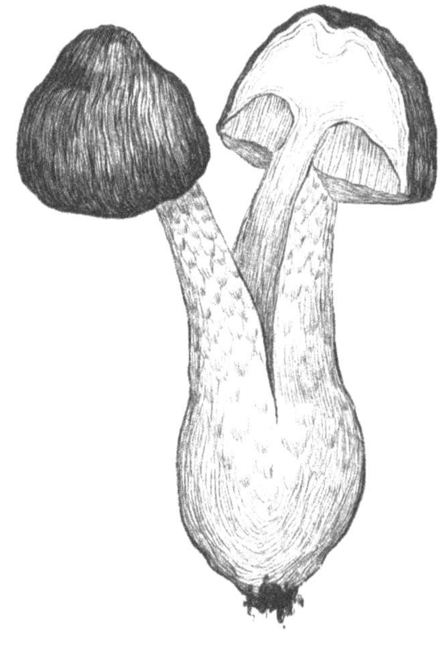

"You got more," the generous-hearted Valya would sing out.

"But look at yours. They don't get any better than that."

Tolya would stroke his wife's damp, sweaty back and take from his faithful old duffel bag a half-pint of vodka, some boiled eggs, and a little slab of lard rubbed with garlic, that had tobacco flakes sticking to its pink flank, and they would feast, with an occasional glance at the stingy fall sun. And it might be that they'd tumble to the ground, doing as young people do, in the pleasant shade of the late-year foliage, until the spiteful little black ants started harassing them, biting them all over their tender spots, so thoroughly that for a week afterward they couldn't so much as dream of sitting down.

But oh, the old days, those sweet old days, are long gone, and the Konoplyannikovs, two halves that had been a whole, prowl the woods on their lonesome, and it gives Granny Valya no joy to find a sturdy-legged boletus, and Grandpa Tolya has no use anymore for a Caesar's mushroom. They begrudgingly cram into their baskets whatever comes to hand – a family of red-headed chanterelles, a gray milk cap – and they aren't even too squeamish to pick those runny-nosed rough-stemmed boletes or a clutch of identical honey mushrooms with spotted caps. There's no zest in it, there's no love, there's nothing but the mean-spirited moodiness that drives them into the forest for no apparent reason than to mock all that had been good about their life together.

And so they wander, walking in circles, and Grandpa Tolya sees Valya's scarlet shirt flickering amid the birches, and Granny Valya hears Tolya groaning as he straightens up, and realizes that his back has stiffened again and thinks, out of old habit, that he needs to go to the healer woman to have the lumbago beat out of him, because that's helped before... And the old man wants so much to hug that fool of an old woman, and grab a big handful of a soft rump snugly tucked into old sweatpants, and tumble her to the ground again under the same spruces that long ago had shot up to become slender beauties...

But no. They come out of the forest at the same time, and Granny Valya makes a wry face and says, "You've picked some death caps," to which Grandpa Tolya replies, "You're a death cap, Valya. One bite's all it takes to poison a man," and she follows up with, "An old toadstool like him is good for nothing but steeping in store-bought vodka to cure the arthritis..." And they go their separate ways, into a new and lonely life where even mushrooms bring no pleasure.

THE AUTHOR'S STORY

Varvara Buzina's family history may sound like a figment of someone's imagination, but it isn't. The simple fact is that the lives and fates of those who came before her, as the nineteenth century collided with the twentieth, were a catalogue of adventures, but usually not enjoyable ones.

Varvara's great-grandfather was an impoverished nobleman who by the end of the 1800s owned only one estate that wasn't mortgaged to the hilt, in Pskov Province. His wife, Varvara Ilinichna, died in childbirth, leaving two sons and a daughter motherless. Nikolai, the oldest son, an ambitious and driven individual, graduated from the Pskov Cadet Academy, and set off to conquer St. Petersburg and pursue a military career. Daughter Yelena married, but that marriage was a failure. Her husband was a gambler who squandered her fortune, such as it was, and ultimately drank himself to death. The weak and timid Alexei, the youngest son, who had, by no fault of his own, caused his mother's death, stayed with his father until the latter died.

Nikolai saw combat in the disastrous Russo-Japanese War of 1904 and 1905, and was holding the rank of colonel by the time the First World War broke out. He was wounded in one of the many battles he fought in that war. Then, wanting no part of the Russian Revolution of 1917, he joined the anti-Bolshevik White Army. After the White forces' crushing defeat on the River Don, he fled, was again wounded, and was saved and nursed back to health by Agafya, a peasant woman from a small Cossack village who belonged to the traditionalist religious group known as the Old Believers.

Praskovya, Agafya's daughter, fell in love with Nikolai, but neighbors informed on them, and Nikolai was shot as a traitor to the Bolshevik cause. Praskovya fled her village with her newborn son. On the open road, she contacted a fatal case of typhus, abandoned the child on the outskirts of the nearest town, and died. Her son was declared a foundling and placed in an orphanage, where he was named Igor and given the last name Buzina, which means "elderberry," because he had been discovered under an elderberry bush.

Igor inherited the personality of the father he'd never known. He studied hard and enrolled at the University of Leningrad to study history in 1940, just before Germany invaded Russia. He left academia to join the Red Army as a volunteer, was wounded in July 1944 near Pskov, and found himself in a temporary military hospital located, of all places, in the grounds of his ancestral estate – or what was left of it. To Igor, though, this was nothing more than a place for him to heal.

Strange things began happening there. The old man who kept the furnace stoked was always peering at him, asking him where he was from and who his people were. Igor, of course, could tell him nothing. And then, while one of the nurses, who also happened to be the stoker's wife, was dressing Igor's wound, she saw on his back a birthmark she recognized.

The stoker had served as an orderly to Nikolai, Igor's father, toward the end of his military career, and his wife had been there to help Praskovya as she was giving birth to Igor. After Praskovya was forced to flee with her little one, the couple had long looked for the two but without success. Igor, meanwhile, was growing into the image of his father, which is what had initially caught the stoker's eye.

The recuperating Igor began exploring the mansion's abandoned, looted library, finding old photographs, books, and documents that brought his family history into even closer focus and made him determined to return to Pskov after the war to continue investigating. The mystery of Igor Buzina's lineage was a mystery no more. But, those being complicated times, he shared his discovery with no one, not even his young wife, Natalya. The years passed, the danger receded, and Igor at last told his secret to their daughter – named Varvara, in honor of Igor's grandmother – shortly before his death.

Varvara graduated from the village school with honors, went off to Moscow, and was accepted into a theater institute there. She landed some stage and screen roles but never found fame, and began to think about going back to the village. Her husband was categorically against the idea, her friends and colleagues tried to dissuade her, but Varvara felt that only in a quiet place, amid forests and fields, would she be genuinely happy.

For thirty years she has lived almost within sight of the ruined mansion that had been home to so many generations of her forebears. Like everyone else in the village, she runs her modest household, keeps a cow and some chickens, grows vegetables, and prowls the forest gathering mushrooms and berries. And that's all here, in her book. Varvara pens stories about her neighbors, the local dogs and cats, the artless life of the Russian countryside. Her dream is to one day sit down and write her family's history, an epic tale that has only been touched on here.